Palmer Patch

Palmer Patch

Barbara Brooks Wallace

Illustrated by Lawrence DiFiori

Follett Publishing Company
Chicago

ISBN 0–695–40668–X   Titan binding
ISBN 0–695–80668–8   Trade binding

Library of Congress Catalog Card Number: 76–2185

23456789/8281807978

From beginning to end,
this book belongs to
my husband Jim.

Contents

I/ *The New Animal*   9

II/ *The Worry*   16

III/ *The Kittens*   28

IV/ *The Decision*   44

V/ *The Swinging Gate*   55

VI/ *The Mistake*   59

VII/ *The Fair*   66

VIII/ *The Egg*   75

IX/ *The Barn*   80

X/ *The Strange Animal*   89

XI/ *The Forest*   98

XII/ *The Attack*   105

XIII/ *The Last Decision*   113

XIV/ *The Ending*   117

I / The New Animal

Whether it arrives by
invitation or by accident,
by birth or by box, the
coming of a new animal is
a joyful thing.

From THE THOUGHTS OF CLYDE

Jonathan Patch brought the new animal from the pet shop in a large brown cardboard box. He set the box carefully down on its side on the driveway, just inside the white fence that enclosed the backyard. "I'll be right back, Palmer. Don't be frightened," he whispered softly into the box. Then he raced toward the house.

"Mother, Dad, I've got him!" he yelled excitedly. A moment later, the door to the screen porch had slammed shut, and Jonathan had disappeared into the house.

Resting quietly under the shade of a tall, spreading sycamore tree in the middle of the backyard, a goat, two dogs, and a cat looked curiously at one another, and then at the box sitting forlornly on the driveway, its flaps partly open. The only sound in the hot summer air came from a bee buzzing near a patch of pink geraniums over by the white frame garage.

Suddenly, the two dogs stood up and loped silently toward the box. The cat padded along behind them, and the goat followed her at a slower, more dignified pace. The goat and the cat stopped a few feet from the box, but the dogs went right up and began to sniff it.

Inside the hot, dark box, Palmer shifted uneasily as first one black nose and then another appeared at the narrow opening.

Sniff! Sniff, sniff, sniff! The noses of the two dogs moved swiftly and surely over the flaps of the box.

Palmer could hear his own heart pounding. Could *they?* he wondered.

The smaller dog whined anxiously. "It's not an animal I've ever smelled before, Clyde. Have you?"

"I'm afraid not, Fringe," replied Clyde's deep voice. "What do you make of it, Scratch?"

Palmer saw the two black noses of Clyde and Fringe replaced by the pink nose of a cat, who sniffed daintily, but just as surely, up and down the opening of the box. "The smell means nothing to me," Scratch said. "Jonathan should have told us what the new animal is. I hate surprises. Why, for all we know, there's nothing in that box but an egg."

"Egg? Egg?" An excited voice drew near the box. "Did someone say *egg?* Is it in the box? Is it for me?" A duck's face pushed its way suddenly into the box and stared at Palmer. Palmer wasn't certain what to make of the duck, so he simply stared back. The face withdrew rapidly.

"Mercy! It isn't an egg at all! It's something big and black with a great bushy tail. Is someone playing a joke on me? A body can't even long for an egg these days without someone making something out of it!" The duck began to quack and wail and beat her wings up and down.

"There, there, Mrs. Alabaster!" Clyde said. "It isn't a joke at all. This is the new animal Jonathan told us about. It's just arrived."

"Mercy!" said Mrs. Alabaster, quieting down. "Has it come out yet? Does anyone know what it is?"

"No to both questions," said Scratch wearily.

Inside the box, Palmer heard the sound of feathers being plumped out and Mrs. Alabaster settling comfortably down on the driveway. "Socrates, why don't you just invite him out?" she asked.

"A splendid suggestion, Mrs. Alabaster," replied the voice of Socrates. Palmer heard hoofs trotting up to his box. "Good animal," Socrates said, "will you be so kind as to leave the box?"

Palmer moved as far back against the box as he could go.

Socrates spoke again. "I would like to suggest, whoever you are, that if you don't appear soon, I shall have to demolish the box in which you are encased."

"Good grief, Socrates!" snorted Scratch. "What he means, you there in the box, is that if you don't come out, he's going to eat it!" She hissed angrily.

Palmer didn't budge.

"Very well then," said Socrates with a sigh. He took a loud crunching bite out of the cardboard flaps.

With his shelter rapidly disappearing from around him, there wasn't much left for Palmer to do. He inched forward.

Socrates took a second bite, bigger and crunchier than the first.

The box creaked as Palmer inched, and inched again. Then slowly, carefully, wondering which of his next steps would be the last, Palmer inched out. A half circle of animal faces stared at him curiously.

A dust-colored goat stood serenely in the cen-

ter, his jaw still rotating over a piece of brown cardboard. A white duck peered inquisitively from behind the goat's legs. To one side, a large striped gray cat with a gleaming white fur bib sat calmly washing her face and casting secret glances over her paws. Opposite her stood two dogs. One was large and golden tan, with a thick body, a solid square head, and soft brown eyes. The second, who barely reached the large dog's stomach, blinked at Palmer with bright eyes that were nearly hidden behind a curtain of sandy, gray-brown hair. Both dogs' tails were wagging furiously.

At once, the dogs padded toward Palmer. He stood perfectly still as they explored him thoroughly with moist black noses, but inside he was trembling. Would they discover that somehow, somewhere, his only weapon had stopped working, and that he was helpless? The two finished their examination and padded back to their places in the circle.

Scratch stopped washing her face for a moment. "What exactly are you?" she asked, her whiskers twitching.

Palmer hesitated. "I'm—I'm a skunk."

"Mercy!" exclaimed Mrs. Alabaster. "What's that?"

"I'm from the forest," Palmer replied simply, thinking it ought to explain everything.

But the others all looked at him blankly.

"Have you a name?" asked Socrates.

Palmer thought a moment. He had been given his name only a very short while ago when Jonathan whispered to him through the crack in the box, and it was still strange to him. He wondered if he could even say it.

"I—I guess it's Palmer," he stammered.

And he knew that thinking of himself as Palmer was only the first of a whole string of new things he was going to have to learn about this new place and these strange new animals. Probably a much longer string than they were going to have to learn about him.

II / *The Worry*

*An animal's best interests
are served in the kitchen.*

From THE THOUGHTS OF SCRATCH

Palmer awoke early to the sound of the
screen door slamming. He had been in his new
home only three days, but already he knew what
the sound meant without stopping to think about it.
It meant that some member of the Patch family had
come from the house to fill his bowl with breakfast.

Palmer had never been in the house, but he had
heard all about it from the two dogs, Clyde and
Fringe. Inside, they reported eagerly, there were
dozens of worn places on chairs where cats had
been allowed to nap; old tennis balls under tables

for dogs to chase and chew; comfortable baskets filled with well-worn blankets; a bowl of scraps always in the refrigerator, often along with a magnificent steak bone in a paper sack (brought home for the dogs the night before from a dinner party); a veterinarian's telephone number right under the name of the family doctor; pans of water; bowls of milk; and hair on *everything*. From the way the dogs talked, it sounded like some kind of animal heaven. Palmer, however, soon tired of hearing about it. As a skunk, his domain didn't include the inside of the house, so all he was really interested in was the backyard, and he already knew all he needed to know about that.

On his very first day, he had discovered the exact backyard location of three large bowls always filled with fresh water. A red pottery bowl lay at the foot of an old weathered-oak ladder that leaned against the garage. A battered tin bowl sat right outside the big green doghouse shared by Clyde and Fringe. And a third bowl, yellow plastic with the picture of two dogs and a cat on it in red, was just under the steps that led to the screen porch.

Palmer had also learned that just about the time he would begin to feel really hungry, somebody always appeared through the screen door to put food in his own little white enamel bowl. It sat outside his pen, an orange-crate lean-to that Jonathan had built up against the garage.

And Palmer was rapidly beginning to learn from all the other animals the meaning of such things as feed sacks, biscuits in boxes, fish and beef in cans, garbage, can openers, and the squeak made by the door of the old refrigerator on the screen porch when it was being opened.

"*I* can hear it at fifty paces outside the fence!" Scratch boasted.

As for his old eating habits, Palmer discovered that there was only one he would have to sacrifice.

"How *did* you find bugs and beetles in the forest where you came from?" Mrs. Alabaster asked him one day.

"Like this," replied Palmer, snuffling about in the dry dust.

"Mercy! I know how to do that," said Mrs. Alabaster proudly.

Then Palmer thrust his nose into a clump of grass. "And this is how I found eggs," he said.

"Eggs!" shrieked Mrs. Alabaster. "Oh, mercy, do you eat eggs?"

"I—I did once," stammered Palmer.

"Oh, mercy!" moaned Mrs. Alabaster. "Once an egg eater, always an egg eater. You've probably had a d—d—duck egg!"

"Mrs. Alabaster," said Palmer, "you are the first duck I have ever known. I have never eaten a duck egg, and I will never eat one."

It was an easy promise for Palmer to make. The

foolish creature had never even produced an egg. Besides that, with all the delicious new taste treats appearing in his bowl almost any time he arrived at it, why bother with eggs? It wasn't really such a big sacrifice.

Now, as he left his pen, Palmer saw that some-one had already dished out breakfast and disappeared back into the house, leaving the screen door trembling on its hinges. Clyde, Fringe, and Scratch were attacking the food in their own bowls outside the porch, and Socrates stood at his trough, gazing thoughtfully out into space. From his jaws hung the limp green leaves of a stalk of celery, going round and round like a lazy revolving fan. Dust flew up in little clouds around them all where Mrs. Alabaster pecked at her feed. Moments later, Palmer had his nose buried in a heap of fragrant garbage and refrigerator scraps. He ended his meal by licking a delicious bit of greasy bacon rind from the edge of his bowl, and then started out for the place in the backyard he had been visiting every morning.

"Hey, where are you going?" Clyde called out to him.

"Oh, just behind the garage," Palmer replied carelessly.

"Well sir, it does seem to me that you spend an awful lot of time behind that garage," said Clyde, loping over to him. "What is it you do back there?"

The other animals began strolling over closer to them because it looked as if something interesting might be going on.

"Nothing much," Palmer said. "Nap a little. Root around in the dust. Nothing much."

"That's not all he does!" Scratch said, humping her back and opening her mouth in a wide yawn. "I've seen him. He arches his tail, backs into the garage, then does some funny little dance. It looks odd to me." She began to wash her whiskers sleepily.

"It isn't a funny little dance at all!" Palmer burst out huffily. "And there's nothing odd about trying to get a weapon to work."

In the silence that followed this outburst, Palmer could almost hear his words drop on the ground like hard pebbles. He knew that he had fallen into a trap. All the animals stared at him curiously.

"What kind of weapon is that?" asked Scratch, studying Palmer through half-closed eyelids. "It certainly couldn't have anything to do with claws." She unsheathed her own and examined them with pride.

Palmer stared stiffly at the ground. "No, it's —it's smell," he said.

Mrs. Alabaster uttered a relieved quack. "Mercy, we're all used to that around here! Smells are nothing new to *us*."

"This one would be," Palmer said flatly.

"Show us! Show us! Clyde, make him show us!" Fringe said excitedly.

"Well sir," Clyde said, pausing to attend to a flea at the base of his tail, "whether or not Palmer shows us is up to *him*."

"In the interest of increasing knowledge and the betterment of everything, we would be grateful if you would endeavor to demonstrate this weapon of yours, Palmer. Who knows what we might learn from it," said Socrates.

"What he means," purred Scratch, "is that we're all curious." She cast a gleaming sideways look at Socrates, who simply picked up the remains of a peanut-butter-flavored paper napkin and chewed it in stately silence.

For moments, there was only the sound of his jaw going round and round over the napkin. "I can't show you," Palmer said at last, slowly and carefully. "I'm not ready yet."

Scratch's tail sliced through the air. "Ha! What you mean is that you can't, period. Isn't that it?"

"No, it isn't!" Palmer blurted out.

"Prove it!" hissed Scratch.

"Well, all right then, I *will* show you!" Palmer cried. "But you'll be sorry. Don't say I didn't warn you!"

No one even flinched. It was just as Mrs. Ala-

baster had said. The animals were used to smells, and to them it would be just a new variety, that was all.

Up until the last moment, Palmer was determined to put on a brave front. After all, perhaps his weapon would work that day. He felt he was just upset enough and *frightened enough* for it to work. "All right, here goes!" he said.

Slowly, he backed up to the sycamore tree. Deliberately, he arched his tail. "One, two, three—go!"

Nothing happened.

"Go!" said Palmer again.

Still nothing happened.

The animals looked politely interested, but they had begun to fidget.

"Well?" said Scratch.

"All right, so it's gone!" Palmer cried out. "I've known it all along. I just hoped it wasn't, that's all."

"Are you sure?" Clyde asked.

"Well, do you notice anything different about the air?" Palmer said gloomily.

The animals all raised their noses and sniffed, but there was nothing in the summer air except the old familiar aromas of the backyard, the scent of goat standing out a little more than the rest.

Scratch unsheathed her claws, stared at them a moment, then quickly drew them in again. "When

did you use your weapon last?" she asked with
narrowed eyes.

"In a box when I was captured in the forest,"
said Palmer. "After that, I was carried someplace
and went to sleep for a time. When I woke up in a
cage, I tried to use my weapon again, but it was
gone. While I was sleeping, human beings stole it!"

Clyde exchanged knowing glances with Fringe.
"Why, Palmer, they didn't steal it at all. They
simply took it!" Clyde looked as pleased as if he
had just chased after an old stick and discovered it
was a steak bone.

"So what's the difference?" asked Palmer.

"The difference," Clyde said triumphantly, "is
that it was done for your own good! Why, it's—
it's like *baths*."

"Baths?" questioned Palmer dismally. "What
have baths got to do with anything?"

"Well sir," said Clyde, "Fringe and I hate it
when we have to have a bath, but we stand still and
put up with all that flea soap and scrubbing because we know it's for our own good. Makes us
smell a lot nicer."

Smell a lot nicer! To *whom?* thought Palmer.
Certainly not to the dogs! From the foolish, ador-
ing look on Clyde's face, it was clear that this
thought had never even occurred to him. However,
Palmer saw no point in bringing it up. He would
only be opening up a whole new batch of ridicu-

lous backyard animal reasoning if he did, and he wanted to stick with his own pressing problem.

"I don't care!" he finally exploded. "I don't see anything good about not being able to protect myself."

Clyde looked surprised at this outburst. "Why, you have the Patch family to protect you now," he said gently.

"Once you've been taken in by the Patch family, they'll protect you forever," said Socrates, his beard shaking with emotion.

"They feel responsible for you," said Clyde.

"They love you," said Fringe.

"Even if you don't have eggs!" said Mrs. Alabaster.

"And even if you *do* have kittens!" said Scratch, with surprising feeling in her voice.

But all Palmer could think about in the end was what Clyde had said—it was done for his own good. What did Clyde know, foolish, trusting backyard animal, with his waving tail and his drooling doggy love? How could any of them know what it felt like for a forest-born-and-bred animal to lose his only means of protection, his precious weapon?

Palmer went right to his pen where he sat in gloom the rest of the day. He wouldn't even come out when Jonathan brought his best friend, Harold Miller, to see him.

"He just sits in there," Jonathan said to Harold.

"I don't understand why he doesn't want to come out."

"I don't either," said Harold, peering into Palmer's pen. "You know, that's a terrible pen, Jonathan. I thought you were going to build him a new one."

"I was," Jonathan replied, "but I decided to wait. You know, we aren't sure what's going to happen." He raised an eyebrow at Harold.

"Oh, that's right," said Harold.

Inside the pen, Palmer shivered. Something going to happen? To *him*? Something worse than what had already happened? He huddled even more tightly against the back of his pen.

Later, Jonathan dragged his mother out to look at Palmer. Mrs. Patch arrived all covered with yellow paint drips from painting the basement ceiling. She peered into the pen, too.

"I don't know, Jonathan," she said doubtfully. "He *looks* all right. His coat is black and glossy. His tail is bushy. Of course, I have no idea how you tell if a skunk is sick—whether you feel his nose or something like that. Well," she concluded with a sigh, "if he's not chirpier by tomorrow, we'll take him over to Dr. Wimple."

But shortly after the screen door banged that evening, Palmer emerged and ate a substantial dinner of potato skins, some Friskies dog dinner, a lettuce stalk, and the tag end of a can of pressed ham before disappearing back into his pen.

"I guess we won't have to take him to Dr. Wimple after all," Mrs. Patch said. "We'll just leave him alone. I'm sure he'll get over it."

The animals decided that Mrs. Patch was right.

"He'll come out soon enough when he stops feeling sorry for himself," Scratch said. "I wouldn't waste my time trying to coax him out if I were you." With a flick of her tail, she made a brisk exit over the fence.

That night thunder shook the sky. Lightning hurled eerie shadows through the leaves of the sycamore tree, and rain came down in dark flapping sheets. In the morning, the backyard was filled with the kind of crystal silence that often comes after a rain. Later, the sky turned a brilliant blue, and a hot, bright sun came out. So, at last, did Palmer. But it was only because staying cooped up in his pen proved too dismal and boring, and there was nothing that said you had to be miserable *and* uncomfortable at the same time. Still, he stayed strictly to himself, refusing to have much to do with either the animals or the Patch family.

III / *The Kittens*

*My dear friends, it is
an absolute, known fact
that kittens and children
go together.*

From THE THOUGHTS OF SOCRATES

The Patch backyard was always filled with Jonathan's friends, especially in the summer. They played ball with Clyde and Fringe. They poured water from the garden hose into the animals' drinking bowls. They swung on the rubber tire that hung by a long, thick rope from a branch of the sycamore tree, trailing their sneakers in the dust. They drank cold drinks and let any interested animal lick drops from the bottoms of their Dixie cups. Or they just lay around in the shade, looking up into the tall tree that caught the sunshine on its leaves miles and miles over their heads, rubbing an animal's ear, and talking about all the things they were going to do that summer, but probably never would. But mostly there was the screen door slamming and the refrigerator door squeaking as boys and girls trailed endlessly in and out of the porch bearing paper plates of thick slices of Mr. Patch's butterscotch cake, platters of Mrs. Patch's raisin cookies, pitchers of ice-cold orange punch, and freezers-full of homemade peach ice cream, churned by Jonathan.

Palmer knew that he was missing a lot, but he didn't care. He stayed behind the garage by himself, or sat against the fence off in a corner someplace, or just lay in his pen and moped.

"I thought you said Palmer wasn't sick," he overheard Harold saying to Jonathan one day as the two boys lay on their backs lazily sailing folded paper missiles up into the air.

"We don't think he is," replied Jonathan. "He eats enough for a horse, or a healthy skunk, anyway."

"How do you know how much a healthy skunk eats?" asked Harold. "Anyway, how much you eat doesn't always mean anything. I ate enough for a healthy boy when I had infected tonsils. Maybe Palmer has infected tonsils, Jonathan. Have you looked at them?"

Jonathan groaned. "Nobody goes around looking at a skunk's tonsils, Harold."

"They ought to," said Harold. "They might be missing something."

Jonathan didn't bother to reply to this.

"Well, I thought skunks were supposed to make good pets," Harold continued.

"They do," said Jonathan.

"Then I guess you just got a lemon," said Harold helpfully. "I've never seen such an unfriendly pet. He's always off by himself someplace. I really would look at his tonsils if I were you."

Jonathan shrugged and sighed. "Maybe you're right, Harold."

Palmer sniffed. Look at his tonsils, indeed! That was hardly something that would encourage someone to show his face around the backyard. Palmer remained huddled miserably under Mr. Patch's prize Crimson Glory rosebush in the corner of the yard, and later retreated hurriedly to his pen.

Only at night, when Harold and the other boys and girls had gone home, and the rest of the animals were asleep; when the moon shone down on crumpled Dixie cups and gleamed off a stray spoon lying forgotten in the dust; when the only sounds in the backyard were those of two crickets singing summer songs to one another under the screen porch, would Palmer appear. Sunk deep in gloom, he wandered about the yard, picking up a few crumbs of butterscotch cake, a dusty raisin, or whatever else edible he could find to soothe himself.

Late one night, Palmer left his pen to take his usual stroll about the backyard. The air felt hot and heavy, as if it were going to rain again. But there was another feeling, too, as if something strange and different were going to happen. Clyde and Fringe were not in their doghouse or in the screen porch. They lay under the sycamore tree, their chins resting on their paws, their eyes wide open and alert. Socrates stood near them chewing on a sticky paper plate. His beard swished back and forth through the air with an anxious kind of rhythm, as if he were marking time. Every so often, Mrs. Alabaster's head poked through the door of her pen. She seemed as restless as the others. Why were they all behaving this way? Palmer wondered. He plodded over to the fence and thumped down against it.

All at once, Clyde jumped up and loped over to the door of the toolshed. He stood there for a moment with head tilted, listening, and then turned and bounded toward the house. "Now! Now!" he barked excitedly.

Fringe jumped up, and both dogs leaped at the screen door, whining and pawing at it. Socrates trotted quickly up to them.

"My dear fellows," he said, "you'll have to do better than that. Louder! Louder! You'll never wake them."

The dogs began to bark.

Lights came on in the kitchen, and within moments, Mr. Patch and Jonathan, both in pajamas and slippers, came through the screen door. Jonathan carried a flashlight, and Mr. Patch an open umbrella, because a few raindrops had begun to fall. Palmer watched curiously as Mr. Patch, Jonathan, Clyde, Fringe, and Socrates all marched to the toolshed. Mr. Patch and Jonathan hurried right in, leaving Clyde, Fringe, and Socrates standing outside. Both dogs stood patiently by the closed door, but Socrates paced anxiously up and down as if a bee were attacking his tail.

The raindrops began to patter annoyingly on Palmer's nose, but his curiosity was too great to allow him to return to his pen. Then, to his surprise, Mrs. Alabaster waddled up suddenly and dropped down beside him.

"Mercy! Isn't this exciting?" she said.

"Isn't what exciting?" asked Palmer.

Mrs. Alabaster gave a surprised quack. "You mean you don't know yet?"

"No, I don't!" snapped Palmer.

"Well, you'll find out soon," said Mrs. Alabaster primly.

Bother finding out! thought Palmer. But he stayed around anyway.

Still, he was feeling crosser and crosser, and he was getting wetter and wetter. He was about ready to give up and return to his pen, when the toolshed door flew open, and Mr. Patch and Jonathan stepped out.

"I am happy to announce," said Mr. Patch, addressing the animals, "that Scratch has had her kittens—five to be exact, three girls and two boys! I am sure that you will all want to go in and congratulate her." He snapped open his umbrella, and with the light from Jonathan's flashlight dancing on the path like a giant firefly, the two of them tramped off to the house.

They had no sooner disappeared than Socrates leaped over to Palmer and Mrs. Alabaster. "Think of it!" he said proudly. "Scratch has had her kittens!"

After this, he turned and galloped back to the toolshed, where Clyde and Fringe stood waiting for him to go through the door first, as if this special privilege had always been reserved for him.

Why should Socrates be so joyful about Scratch having kittens? Palmer asked himself. Weren't they the two who were always picking at one another? There was really no explaining the ways of these backyard animals.

Drops of water flew out around Mrs. Alabaster as she rose, gave her rear end a shake, and waddled off toward the toolshed. However, she hadn't gone far when she turned back to Palmer.

"Mercy, Palmer!" she said with surprise. "Aren't you coming to see them?"

Palmer hadn't had any intention of going anywhere except back to his pen to mope, but curiosity got the better of him again. It was hard to believe, but he had never seen a baby animal before, not a baby of any forest creature, not even a baby skunk. He wondered what a kitten looked like.

"I guess I will," he said, trying not to sound too interested, and started out slowly behind Mrs. Alabaster.

The rain had stopped pattering on the sycamore leaves quite suddenly, and from behind a cloud, the moon came like a pale round lantern to light up the garden. By the time Palmer arrived at the toolshed, a gentle beam of moonlight shone through the door and fell softly on odd shapes that turned out to be nothing more mysterious than a jumbled stack of flowerpots, rakes and shovels leaning tipsily against a lawn mower, half-empty bags of peat moss and garden fertilizer, and a potting table strewn with mismatched garden gloves and empty seed packets. Under this table was an old laundry basket lined with a torn pink blanket. And on the blanket

lay Scratch, busily licking a cluster of wriggling, mewing bits of life, none bigger than a small fuzzy peach, with tails like stems, and tiny pink noses, ears, and tight-shut eyes.

Alone outside the circle of animals, Palmer stood absolutely still, gazing spellbound into the basket. He couldn't believe what he was seeing. He wished that he could stay there all the rest of the night, watching these tiny newborn creatures, five helpless little strangers who, like himself, had just come to live in the Patch backyard.

The very next morning, streams of children began arriving at the Patch backyard, and all of them ran at once to the toolshed to visit the new family. With the help of his friends, Jonathan soon had names for all the kittens, which were Clancy, Clarence, Candy, Chris, and Cleopatra, who in a very short time became simply Little Cleo.

Palmer found it almost impossible to stay away from the toolshed himself, but he arranged to go into it only when Mr. and Mrs. Patch, Jonathan and his friends, and all of the other animals were not there. He even made certain that Scratch was asleep when he came to visit. Then he would go over to just sit quietly by the basket and stare into it.

The toolshed was hot, and the air was pungent with the good rich smells of peat moss and fertilizer and warm kittens. Sunshine poured through the window, lighting up a shaft of dreamy, drifting particles of dust. Sometimes, when both Scratch *and* her kittens were asleep, there was nothing moving in the shed but a silent spider weaving its web in an abandoned flowerpot. Palmer loved being in this gentle, peaceful place, and it was he who in the end was sitting there at the splendid moment when the first kitten opened its eyes. He rather hoped things could go on in this quiet way forever, but of course they couldn't, and at last the kittens wobbled out of the basket.

Then one day he arrived at the toolshed door to be met by a kitten coming in the opposite direction. The startled ball of fur suddenly puffed out, arched its back furiously, raised its tiny stem of a tail straight up in the air, and hopped away from Palmer in a funny little dancing side-step. When Palmer simply thumped down and remained motionless in the doorway, the kitten came toward him and batted his nose with its paw. The small prickles from its claws surprised Palmer, but he didn't so much as quiver. The kitten stared at him a moment, and then returned to bat his nose again, but this time there were no prickles. Palmer was enchanted. The kitten was Little Cleo, already his favorite. She looked like a miniature Scratch, except she not only had her mother's gray tiger-striped coat and white bib, but four white mittens on her paws as well.

This event was the beginning of a whole new source of wonder and delight for Palmer. All the kittens now came freely in and out of the toolshed, and he would sit for hours watching them chase their shadows, their tails, and each other, collapsing all at once around Scratch in small warm hills, and falling asleep as easily as a butterfly lights on a clover leaf.

Palmer knew at almost any minute of the day where each kitten was. If one was missing for even a moment, he would go in search of it, although it was rare that a kitten *would* be missing. They seemed to be always clustered together somewhere in the toolshed, playing around the roots of the sycamore tree, or sound asleep in the sun outside the toolshed door. One day, however, Palmer noticed that all the kittens except Clarence were by the garage, having an exciting time batting around an old sycamore button-ball one of them had discovered under the geraniums. It wasn't a game any kitten would ordinarily stay away from. Palmer started on a tour of the backyard at once to look for the missing Clarence.

He went twice around the sycamore tree, toured all the pens and even his own favorite napping place behind the garage. In the toolshed, he made a thorough search behind every flowerpot, the rakes and shovels, and the lawn mower. He poked his nose under the potting table and all through the pink blanket in the basket, but there was no sign of the stray kitten.

Growing more anxious, Palmer plodded around the yard once more. He saw Scratch giving herself a good tongue scrubbing in the sunlight by the fence, and she seemed unconcerned about anything except her bath. Though he didn't particularly want to talk to them, Palmer ended up going over to Clyde and Fringe, who were resting in the shade outside the screen door. Both of them looked rather surprised to see him coming toward them.

"Clarence is lost," Palmer whispered anxiously. "He's gone, disappeared, vanished. I've looked everywhere and can't find him. What should we do?"

Fringe turned to Clyde. "Doesn't he know? Doesn't he know, Clyde?" he asked.

Another secret? What was *this* one all about? "Don't I know what?" Palmer snapped.

Little clouds of dust rose up as Clyde smacked his tail on the ground. "Why, that Clarence isn't lost at all," he replied. "He's been taken away."

"Taken away!" cried Palmer, repressing a shriek. "By whom?"

"Why, by one of Jonathan's friends," Clyde said calmly. "You didn't think this cute batch of kittens was going to stay around long with all these children coming to see them, did you?"

"You mean he's been stolen?" said Palmer in a horrified whisper.

"No, no, no!" Clyde's leg went thump! thump! thump! with the words as he attended to a flea behind his ear. "He's been *given* away. Someday they all will be. Clarence is just the first to go, that's all."

All given away! Clarence just the first to go! "That's all!" Palmer exploded. "But who gives them away? Do Jonathan and Mr. and Mrs. Patch know about this?"

"Well sir," drawled Clyde, "who do you think gives them away?"

Palmer felt the fur around his neck rise in horror. "Does—does Scratch know about it?"

"Yes," both dogs replied.

"And doesn't she care?" asked Palmer.

"Well sir," said Clyde, "it isn't so much that she doesn't care as that she can't count. She doesn't really know what's happened until the last kitten goes. Then we all have to be mighty nice to Scratch for a while. She gets over it in time."

"She always has, hasn't she, Clyde?" said Fringe.

"Always has," Clyde replied cheerfully.

Too discouraged to ask any more questions, Palmer crept silently to his pen.

One kitten after another disappeared until finally there was only one left, and that was Little Cleo. Palmer trailed around after her every waking minute, and was scared each time he closed his eyes that he would wake to find her gone. The only reason Little Cleo had not yet been given away was that she was Jonathan's favorite kitten as well as Palmer's.

"Couldn't we keep her a little longer?" Palmer heard Jonathan ask Mrs. Patch one day as they were both in the backyard sanding down blue paint from an old kitchen table.

Mrs. Patch rubbed a test finger over a spot she had been working on, and then replied thoughtfully, "Dear, you know how attached we all become to an animal once we've had it a while. If we keep Little Cleo too long, I'm afraid we'll never be able to part with her, and I just don't think we ought to add another animal to our family, especially not at this time."

"Oh, please, Mom!" Jonathan pleaded. "Only for a few more days."

Mrs. Patch finally smiled. "Oh, well, I suppose a few more days won't hurt anything. But no more than that!"

Especially not at this time? What was that supposed to mean? Palmer asked himself. But he didn't dwell on it long, because the only thing that really mattered was *only for a few more days!* Was that the best he could hope for? How could he bear to have Little Cleo gone? If only there were someone he could talk to about it. And at last he thought of Socrates. Socrates had been more excited than anyone about the arrival of the kittens. What did *he* think of all this?

At the moment, Socrates was standing by his trough, rotating his jaws over a crisp carrot. Palmer hurried over to him to catch him before his mouth could be occupied by another carrot, or stalk of celery, or paper plate.

"Don't *you* care about all the kittens being given away, Socrates?" Palmer asked, sounding almost hysterical.

"Of course I care, my dear fellow!" Socrates said. Then he gazed off into the tree someplace for a moment. "But this is the way it's always been." He spoke as if *that* explained everything.

Palmer felt like shouting back, "Well, just because something's always been, doesn't mean it's always been right, does it?" But he didn't, and he said no more about it to anyone.

His weapon stolen. The kittens stolen. What new horror was in store for them? Palmer thought again about what Jonathan had said—"We aren't sure what's going to happen"—and then about what Mrs. Patch had said—"Especially not at this time." What did those strange statements mean? If only he could talk to one of the other animals about it, but what was the use? *That's the way it's always been. They don't do anything unless it's for your own good.* How could he talk to these blind, trusting backyard animals about anything!

Palmer felt more apart from them than he ever had before. He felt more different, more like a stranger, and more lonely and frightened than when he had sat all alone in that hot, dark cardboard box on the driveway.

IV / *The Decision*

Mercy!

From THE THOUGHTS OF MRS. ALABASTER

"I tell you something is wrong!" Scratch said.

Her tail twitched as she spoke to the other animals, all except Palmer, gathered together for a meeting under the sycamore tree. Palmer was off alone under the Crimson Glory rosebush, gloomily snuffling around in the dust in pursuit of a small black beetle. But he heard every one of Scratch's words hiss through the still summer air. The sound of them made his heart bang suddenly in his chest and a shiver run up his spine.

"Yes, I tell you something's wrong!" Scratch

repeated, drawing back her lips to let a snarl escape through her sharp little teeth. "Just take this afternoon, for instance. Jonathan has trailed through that screen door so many times I think he's wearing out the hinges. Each time he has patted us all on the head, looked glum, then gone back in again. And he hasn't said a word to any of us, not one word. That tells me something's wrong!"

"Oh, bah!" said Socrates.

"Don't you mean *maa*, Socrates?" snapped Scratch.

"When I say *bah*, I mean *bah*!" Socrates snapped back. "And that's bah to something being wrong."

"Well, you can all hide from it if you want to," replied Scratch, bristling, "but I feel it in my bones. You all know a cat has whiskers to keep his head and the rest of him out of small, dangerous places, but a cat has bones to tell him the things his whiskers can't. And my bones definitely tell me something is wrong!"

"Oh, mercy! Something wrong!" quacked Mrs. Alabaster. "Something wrong!" Her wings trembled helplessly as she fell to the ground with a thump.

"Now calm yourself, Mrs. Alabaster," Clyde said. "There's no use going to pieces over this. I believe Scratch has a point, though. None of us knows the meaning of wrong things in the Patch household, but I think we all have to admit that we've been having funny feelings these past few days."

Palmer finally stood up and started on a slow plod toward the others. But as was usual lately, nobody paid any attention to him, so he dropped down a short distance away from them and rubbed his nose glumly on a tree root.

The animals were silent as the thoughts Clyde had put into words trembled in the air around them. Then at last Fringe spoke up timidly.

"Clyde?"

"Yes, Fringe?"

"Clyde, what does 'to be farmed out' mean?"

"Well sir, I don't really know, Fringe," Clyde said. "Where did you hear that?"

"Oh, I was sleeping behind a chair in the living room yesterday, and woke up just in time to hear Mr. Patch say to Jonathan, 'They'll have to be farmed out.'

"Then Jonathan said, 'But they won't understand, Dad.'

"And then Mrs. Patch said, 'Well, there isn't anything else we can do, dear.'

" 'Shouldn't we explain it to them right away?' Jonathan asked.

" 'No, not yet, Jonathan,' Mr. Patch said. 'No sense in getting them all upset. We'll try to keep as calm about this as possible until the last moment.' "

Fringe's head tilted questioningly. "Clyde, do you suppose they were talking about us?"

In an instant, Scratch was on her feet, her eyes flashing. "Of course they were talking about us! And what does 'to be farmed out' mean? I'll tell you what it means. It means that we're all going to be given away, separated, from them and from each other. That's what it means!"

"Oh, mercy!" cried Mrs. Alabaster. "I thought it meant we were going to visit a farm. I was on a farm once, you know," she went on conversationally, as if the other thought were too terrible for her to take in. "Of course, I was only an egg then."

"My dear Mrs. Alabaster," said Socrates, "you were not an egg. You were *in* an egg."

Mrs. Alabaster stiffened. "Well, I don't care!" she said. "When you're in an egg, you *are* an egg. Mercy, I'm tired of having others tell me about eggs!" She sat down in a huff.

"Socrates," said Clyde, a gentle reproof in his voice, "we are not gathered here to discuss what is or isn't an egg. What we are trying to do is to find out what is or isn't going on in the house. If 'farm out' means what Scratch says it means—that we might all be given away separately—then this is a very serious matter."

Suddenly, Mrs. Alabaster threw her head under one wing and began to sob softly. "Mr. Patch said that one day he was going to build a pond in the backyard, an egg-shaped pond just for me. Would he have said that if we were all going to be given away? Mercy, I don't understand any of this!" Her words were muffled in the feathers of her wing.

Despite himself, Palmer felt sorry for Mrs. Alabaster, putting her faith in Mr. Patch, with his twinkling blue eyes and his treacherous human heart. The poor trusting duck!

Clyde turned to her and said softly, "None of us understands this, Mrs. Alabaster. If there were only someone who could explain it to us and answer our questions."

"There is someone!" declared Scratch. "He's a friend of mine, a cat named Max who used to belong to another family. He's only been with his new family a short while. I'll go right now and ask him what he thinks." Before anyone could offer another suggestion, she was over the fence and gone.

They were all silent after she left, each animal deep in its own thoughts. Hardly a whisker, an ear, a tail, or a feather twitched as they sat under the sycamore tree, as quiet and still as if they had all been painted against the backyard. The waiting seemed endless, but at last the lithe silhouette of a cat appeared against the pale blue sky, and

Scratch leaped down from the fence into the yard. She was tense and excited. Her green eyes were wild. Her tail flicked the air like an angry snake.

"It's just what I thought!" she said in a hoarse, dry voice. "Max said it was the same thing with him, all this talk about farming out. The only difference is, when they separated him from the other animals in *his* family, they said they'd come get him one day. One day, ha! They'll never come get him, Max says. They've forgotten all about him; he's certain of it."

Fringe's eyes were bleak as he looked up at Clyde. "I can't be separated from you, Clyde— not ever!"

"Of course you can't," Clyde said. "Nor can any of us be separated from each other. We belong together. That's what I can't understand. Our family knows that, and they wouldn't do anything to hurt us. They never have."

This was more than Palmer could stand. "Never have!" he blurted out. "Never have! What about taking my weapon?" He rose and moved slowly toward the others.

"Our family didn't take it. Some other human beings did," Clyde reminded him gently.

"Well, you haven't noticed ours giving it back, have you?" snorted Palmer. "And how about Scratch's kittens? What's so wonderful about giving them all away? You're all just blind when it comes to the Patch family because you came here when you were babies and you don't know any better!"

The other animals stared ahead without saying anything. For once, the old answers—*that's the way it's always been* and *they don't do anything unless it's for your own good*—didn't make sense.

"But here's something you *ought* to know!" Palmer said, and he went on to tell them about the curious remarks he had overheard Jonathan and Mrs. Patch make.

When Palmer finished, it was as if their solid, dependable sycamore tree had come crashing down in their midst. There seemed to be no question now as to what was going to happen to them.

"But why, friends, *why*?" said Socrates.

Fringe turned anxious eyes to Clyde. "Perhaps they're angry with us. We've all done wrong things, haven't we, Clyde? You and I bury bones in the flower beds all the time, even though Mrs. Patch has warned us not to. Isn't that so, Clyde?"

"Yes, sir, yes, it is," said Clyde. "All of us have done wrong things, and I think we all know what they are."

"I confess that I have developed an insatiable appetite for rose petals in season," Socrates said mournfully. "Mr. Patch has spoken to me about it time and again, but I have persisted in nibbling his prize blossoms right down to the stems!"

Mrs. Alabaster shook her rear end, and several feathers flew out, drifting to the ground like soft summer snowflakes. "There, you see!" she said. "I do that all the time. Jonathan complains about having to clean up my feathers, and my duck feed, and—other things I strew around the back-yard. Mercy! I should have tried to be more careful."

The confessions had now come around the circle to Palmer, but he remained silent. He didn't need to say anything. They all knew he was a lemon. A failure. A flop. A total bust as a pet. There was no mystery about why anyone would be glad to see him go. The only mystery might be why they had got him in the first place. However, Palmer would not have confessed anything anyway. He was too disgusted by these ridiculous backyard animals trying to come up with some soppy reason for this terrible thing being done to them.

The only one of the grown animals besides Palmer who hadn't spoken was Scratch. Her eyes had suddenly turned a cold, hard glass-yellow, with pupils narrowed down to black splinters.

"Well, Little Cleo and I have been told to use our sandbox, and we go right on using any newly-turned flower bed we feel like, but I don't think that's any excuse to get rid of us," she spat out. "It's betrayal, pure and simple!"

Betrayal! The word hit them like a single stinging hailstone.

In the midst of the stunned silence, Fringe spoke up in a small, tentative voice. "They did say they were going to explain it to us. They *did* say that, Clyde. Shouldn't we wait until then?"

"I just don't know, Fringe," Clyde said sadly.

"Well, I do!" Scratch burst out. "I say waiting in this case may be too late. Anyway, waiting for *what?* How does anyone go about explaining betrayal? Palmer could well be right in all he says. He's had something taken away from him, and so have I. The rest of you ought to think about that. What's to say we won't be taken away from each other forever! And what can we do about it then? Maa? Mew? Bark? Quack? Refuse to eat?" Scratch switched her tail angrily.

An even longer silence followed this outburst.

"My dear friends," said Socrates, "I ask you, what can we do about it? What can we do to make certain we all stay together?"

Scratch began to wash her face. She appeared calm, until you looked closely and saw that her paws were trembling. "We can run away," she said softly.

"Run away!" squawked Mrs. Alabaster. She began to flap her wings wildly. "Oh, mercy, run away!"

"Hush, Mrs. Alabaster!" Clyde said sternly. "We don't want to bring the family." He turned to Scratch. "Running away is a terrible thing to consider."

"Well, does anyone have a better idea? Isn't that the only one, when you stop to think about it?" Scratch said.

"Hmmm," muttered Socrates. "It's easy enough for you to say 'run away.' How do you propose that *I* get over the fence? How many flying goats do you know? That would certainly count me out."

"No, it wouldn't count you out, nor any of the rest of us," Clyde said. "Why, the catch on that gate has been loose for months. I discovered it one day by accident, but I never said anything to anyone. Why should I have? Who would have ever needed to know?"

This sad thought caused another silence for a moment.

"Anyway," Clyde went on, "I can get us out with one good swipe at the latch with my paw. That's no problem. The problem is—where would we go?"

They looked at one another in dismay. It was a question none of them had ever thought about. Where *did* animals go when they ran away?

Where? Well, in their case, there was only one place they *could* go to escape from human beings. It was the place that stretched as far as an animal's mind could reach, from somewhere beyond the town to the towering, shadowy mountains miles away. It was the place that promised no warm pens, no regular meals, no water-filled basins, no pond for Mrs. Alabaster. It promised only danger and terror—and each other.

"The forest!" whispered Scratch in a voice so low she could hardly be heard.

Clyde and Fringe whined.

In the whole Patch backyard, there were only the sounds of a dove cooing someplace in the eaves of the house and Mrs. Alabaster crying softly into her wing.

So it was settled.

They would set out that night as soon as the last prying light in the house blinked out. There would be no packing to do, no boxes, no cans, no friendly squeak of the refrigerator door, no one there to care if they left, bidding them a safe journey and a quick return. There would be just themselves, leaving alone and unwanted—watched over only by the night sky, cared about by no one but themselves. Forlorn and dreary, the animals drifted silently to bed that night.

V/The Swinging Gate

*There's a different feeling
going out a gate when you know
you're not coming through it
again.*

From THE THOUGHTS OF SCRATCH

Palmer twisted restlessly in his pen, unable to fall asleep. His heart beat in his chest like a woodpecker attacking a tree stump. He could almost hear it pecking out the words *the forest*. The forest! The forest! He was going back to the forest without his weapon in the company of a band of foolish, trusting, helpless animals. Somewhere along the way, his brains must have flowed out through his ears!

Yet what was the only other choice he had? he asked himself. To stay behind? What did that promise except another box, another dark, lonely trip, and then who knows what? Suppose someday someone grew tired of him and decided to turn him loose in the forest *alone!* No, as long as the others were willing to have him along, he'd have to go with them and just hope they wouldn't desert this gloomy, grousy, moping newcomer in time of danger.

He lay awake, listening to the sighing of the wind in the leaves of the sycamore tree, and smelling for the last time the fragrance of Mr. Patch's prize roses that drifted over to his pen. And as he did, he had one bright thought to give him comfort. Little Cleo had not yet been given away and would come with them. How she would travel on her tiny legs, Palmer could not imagine. But the thought of Little Cleo was the last thing that floated through his mind when, having decided that he would never sleep again, his tired eyes closed at last.

When he awoke, it was to the feel of something warm and wet traveling over his nose. He tried to shake the thing off, but it insisted on following him. Finally, he opened his eyes to see Clyde standing over him, licking his nose with a long pink tongue.

"Come along. It's time," Clyde said. There was no joy in his voice.

The sudden remembrance of what they were about to do jolted Palmer into wide awakeness, and

he hurried from his pen to join the others. How remote the backyard looked in the moonlight, as if they were already miles and miles away from it! How forbidding the tall sycamore tree and the dark house! How strange everything seems when you are leaving it, Palmer thought. Even the leaves on the tree seemed to sway sadly to the sighing of the wind. Palmer remembered how once they had played a lullaby for Scratch's kittens.

The animals walked quietly to the gate and stood there in a silent cluster. Clyde stretched his long, thick, but supple body up to the latch and pushed on it. The gate swung open. Without a sound, the animals walked through one by one. Not a word was said. No one looked back. The gate, swinging gently back and forth in the wind, was the only note they left. The open gate, a messenger without words, would tell Mr. and Mrs. Patch and Jonathan that their animals had left them forever.

VI / *The Mistake*

*Well sir, a dog doesn't want
to lose faith in his nose.
Without it, what is he?*

From THE THOUGHTS OF CLYDE

Traveling single file, they marched silently down the empty street, Clyde first, then Fringe, Little Cleo, Scratch, Mrs. Alabaster, Palmer, and Socrates. But it soon became clear that Little Cleo would have difficulty keeping up with the rest. She was too big now for Scratch to carry in her mouth, so what could they do? They all looked helplessly at one another, for there was no question of leaving Little Cleo behind.

Then Socrates stepped forward. "*I* shall be glad to transport Little Cleo," he said. "A goat's mouth is seldom empty of something, as you well know. I shall simply use the available space for a kitten."

"Well, try not to swallow her," said the kitten's mother calmly.

"My dear Scratch," Socrates returned, "I maintain excellent control of my gullet at all times. Little Cleo will be guarded with my life!"

Carrying a kitten in his mouth would certainly be a sacrifice for a goat with so many opinions, Palmer thought. Clearly it was going to be a time of sacrifice for them all.

Before they had traveled for long, Palmer began to imagine that he felt thirsty and hungry. He thought of the red pottery bowl, the tin bowl, and the yellow plastic bowl filled with cool, clear water in the Patch backyard. He thought of Mrs. Patch's cool, clear voice calling him to supper from the screen door.

Soon he decided that his feet were hurting. Harold had once remarked to Jonathan that Palmer walked as if he were wearing tight shoes. Well, Palmer was certain that that's the way his feet felt right then.

Wouldn't it have been better, he asked himself, to have simply taken a chance on another box, another dark journey to some other human beings who would keep him watered, fed, *and* comfortable? Even if he mistrusted them, wasn't that a better risk than this? What was he doing out here anyway?

But before Palmer could come up with answers to any of his questions, Mrs. Alabaster dropped down suddenly in front of him, and he found himself running into her rear end, nose first.

"Mercy!" she burst out with a great sobbing quack. "Ducks are simply not built for travel. Their legs are too short. Their ends nearly drag on the ground. Mercy! It's a wonder we walk at all!"

"Tut! Tut! Mrs. Alabaster. You are doing splendidly!" said Socrates, forgetting that he had Little Cleo in his mouth and dropping her to the ground with the first "tut." "I am sure we shall find a nice pond for you in the forest." He scooped the kitten back into his mouth without losing a breath.

A pond in the forest? Were the animals going to put their trust in a forest as they once had in human beings? Palmer couldn't believe his ears.

"Hush, hush, everyone!" Clyde warned. "We must be quiet or risk discovery."

No one could argue with this. Except Socrates. "Dear friends," he said sadly, fortunately remembering first to put down Little Cleo, "who would be interested in *us*?"

"Good grief, Socrates!" hissed Scratch. "Who *wouldn't* be interested in the sight of two dogs, a cat, a kitten, a goat, a duck, and a skunk calmly parading down a sidewalk in the middle of the night? Don't be ridiculous!"

Hugging the shrubs and fences that lined the sidewalks, hurrying past treacherous streetlights, they loped and trotted and waddled and plodded along in silence.

Then all at once Clyde's nose went up in the air, and he came to a stop. Sniff! Sniff, sniff! He turned to the others. "Well, it may be that our travels, at least for the night, are over! Palmer, would you or would you not say that that's the forest ahead?"

It surprised Palmer to find that he liked being asked the question by Clyde. It singled him out as the forest expert. He stared ahead importantly.

What he saw certainly looked like a forest. It even smelled like a forest. It did have a kind of neat look about it, a bit too tidy, a bit too trim. Palmer wasn't certain a forest should look so planned. Yet who could say it wasn't a forest, with all those trees?

"Yes, it could be the forest," said Palmer.

"Imagine, the forest already!" exclaimed Mrs. Alabaster.

"Hmmmph!" snapped Scratch. "There is something definitely fishy about this. I've surveyed and studied this neighborhood within an inch of my nine lives. It seems curious to me that I have never noticed a forest practically at my own back door."

"My dear Scratch," declared Socrates, promptly dropping Little Cleo again, "I should certainly think that Palmer would know a forest when he sees one!"

Scratch's tail bristled, but she remained silent.

They arrived at the trees and turned off into them, but they had no sooner passed the first tall elms than Mrs. Alabaster began to shriek. "Mercy, a pond! A pond for me! A pond in the forest!"

It wasn't a pond, actually, yet there *was* a beautiful little pool just ahead of them. In the center of it, a fountain of water gushed from the mouth of a stone deer, making cool, delicious sounds as it splashed into the pool. As the other animals gathered around it to drink, Mrs. Alabaster climbed at once onto the low stone ledge. Soon she was sailing blissfully around the pool, waving to them gaily each time she rounded the stone deer.

Palmer was mystified. It didn't seem to him that a forest would provide such luxuries as a pool with a stone deer in the center. And there was something else bothering him, too. Some very unusual smells had begun wafting into his nose, smells that had nothing to do with a forest, but were much more like ones that followed one of Jonathan's backyard picnics. There was the aroma of potato-salad-on-paper-plate, the fragrance of end-of-hot-dog, the bouquet of bottom-of-ice-cream-cone. And all these heavenly scents came from a green basket not twenty feet from the pool. This certainly was a forest to end all forests, thought Palmer. Still, it was beginning to make him uneasy. The more he thought about it, the more he wished he hadn't been so quick to offer an opinion.

"You know something?" he mumbled at last. "Perhaps Scratch is right. Perhaps this isn't a forest after all."

"Of course I'm right!" Scratch whipped back. "Human! It's a human beings' park; that's what it is. Now I'm certain. I was here once, but I traveled my usual way, through alleys and across backyards, so I didn't recognize it tonight. Forest indeed!" Her eyes flashed with disgust.

"She's right, Clyde. Scratch is right," Fringe said. "You and I have been here with Jonathan, haven't we, Clyde?"

Even Palmer had learned by now what a terrible thing it was for a dog's nose to betray him. Clyde's ears and tail drooped. "I'm sorry," he said gloomily. "I shouldn't have led you here."

Then Scratch surprised Palmer by saying in a kind voice, "Never mind, Clyde. We haven't lost anything by it. I still say there is no compass more true, more accurate, more unfailing, than the nose of a dog. It may be a bit hazy on distance and make a mistake once in a while, but for pinpoint accuracy, give me a dog's nose every time!"

For a cat to make such a statement was a remarkable thing. Clyde's eyes were warm with gratitude. His tail flagged the air. "What do you suggest we do now, Scratch?"

"I say we've been going in the right direction, and we're still in the right direction," Scratch replied. "Keep your nose pointed there, and we'll have it."

There was no need for Scratch or anyone else to say that they could not remain in the park until daylight. Where they would hide when daylight approached was a problem they would have to face when they met it.

After they had all taken another long, cooling drink, and had finally persuaded Mrs. Alabaster that she must leave the pool, they set out once again.

VII / *The Fair*

My dear friends,
the importance of a medal
should not be underestimated,
especially for a goat.

From THE THOUGHTS OF SOCRATES

They were well past the outskirts of town, treading wearily past wide fields and an occasional house that sprang up before them like a menacing night-growing toadstool, when large shadowy shapes appeared suddenly against the sky. It was nearing daybreak, and the shapes could mean the grove of trees they needed to hide in. Tired as the animals were, their steps quickened. But as they drew nearer, the shapes became what they really were—a large cluster of tents.

"And that still means human beings!" snarled

Scratch. "And that means danger. We'll have to keep going."

"Oh, mercy!" said Mrs. Alabaster in a fainting voice.

But all at once Socrates put Little Cleo gently down. "Wait!" he exclaimed. "I smell goat!"

"Well, we've been smelling goat for longer than I care to remember," Scratch said wearily. "What's that got to do with anything?"

"My dear Scratch," replied Socrates, "what I am trying to say is that something abroad in the air tells me there is not just one, but a large number of those splendid animals about. And as you all should know, the presence of a large number of any kind of animal also spells the possible presence of food and shelter."

"Not to mention human beings, Socrates," said Scratch drily.

Clyde raised his nose and took a deep, long sniff. Then he shook his head as if to clear his nose all out again. "No sir, no human beings," he said. "Only goats. Lots of them! They're right in that tent ahead of us, if my nose isn't lying to me. Maybe we should go in and see what we can see."

"Mercy!" said Mrs. Alabaster. "I'm so tired I don't care if I have to sleep right under a goat!"

"What do we do? What do we do, Clyde?" Fringe asked. "Do we just walk in?"

"My dear Fringe," interrupted Socrates, "I shall go in first to announce the rest of you. We should try to preserve the appearance of dignity before these fine creatures. 'Just walk in' indeed!"

As the goat daintily pushed aside the tent flap and trotted in, Palmer couldn't contain a shiver. Once more he wondered what had led him to cast his lot with these ridiculous animals. Good manners at a time like this, when their bodies and feet were sore and aching!

But moments later, Socrates calmly reappeared. "It seems that these goats are in readiness for the judging of themselves this afternoon," he announced. "However, the noble animals bid us welcome and state that we may hide in their tent. The quarters they provide will be crowded, but we will be safe from the prying eyes of human beings."

Clyde's tail swung slowly from side to side. "Tell your good goats that we accept their invitation with pleasure," he said.

Ten or so goats watched politely but curiously from their pens as the Patch animals came one by one through the tent flap. Several of the goats had pushed under their pen gates water bowls and whatever food they had left. Except for Socrates and Palmer, the food wasn't what the rest were used to, but at least there was water. They drank that thirstily and gratefully. When they were finished, Socrates thanked the goats for them all. Then he led them to a pile of fruit and vegetable crates stacked against the tent. Between the wall and the crates was the place where they would have to spend the day.

The goats were certainly right in saying that the quarters would be crowded. When Palmer lay down, a hoof was pressed into his back. Something soft and heavy draped over his tail. The warm, moist air from somebody's nose breathed against his stomach. His own nose was somehow tangled in the feathers of Mrs. Alabaster's rear end. And over all this hung the pungent, pervasive aroma of goat. But nobody cared. They were too exhausted, and within moments after they had somehow settled their tired bodies around one another, they were all sound asleep.

Feathers tickling his nose woke Palmer some time in the late afternoon. They belonged to Mrs. Alabaster, who had stood up and was giving her rear end a slow, shuddering shake. Moments later, the others were also yawning and stretching and trying to stand up in the tight quarters.

Then, suddenly, Clyde stiffened and growled. "Where's Socrates?"

"Oh, mercy! Socrates is missing!" cried Mrs. Alabaster.

"Now hush, Mrs. Alabaster," said Clyde. "He can't be far off."

Scratch bit at a claw. "He'd better not be! If he's been foolish enough to go visiting, he's on his own."

But before another word could be said on the subject, a sudden commotion arose in the tent. Quickly, they all peered through the cracks in the crates to see what was happening.

The goats were trotting briskly out of their pens and down the aisle, each led by a man or woman. And who was right in the middle of them all but Socrates! There was a great deal of jostling and crowding, and in the confusion, no one seemed to notice that he was not being led by anyone. Soon, the tent was emptied of every last goat.

"What in the name of everything animal is he doing?" hissed Scratch.

"Could we see what's happening to Socrates? Could we, Clyde?" Fringe asked anxiously.

"Well sir, don't see how we can, Fringe," Clyde said. "It's too dangerous to go poking our noses out of here. If we got spotted, we'd be finished. We'll just have to wait and see what happens, and we'll just have to hope Socrates doesn't get himself caught and locked up in a pen—or worse!"

"Well, waiting's not my game," Scratch said. "I intend to see what's going on!" With that, she made a sudden leap, and on silent paws that seemed hardly to touch the wooden boxes, flew up to the topmost apple crate, where her sharp eyes had found a small opening in the tent. "Anyway, *someone's* got to keep an eye on that old goat!" they heard her mutter.

"Could you give us a report from up there?" Clyde called to her.

"There's not much to report yet," Scratch replied. "They're all just walking along now, heading for some kind of platform with three human beings on it."

"What's Socrates doing?" asked Clyde.

"He's just going along sedately at the end of the line with the rest," Scratch replied. She paused a moment. "Now they've all reached the platform."

The animals listened closely while Scratch, from her vantage point, went on to report how each goat was led up onto the platform, one at a time, to be examined by two women and a man who were already up there. Then, finally, Socrates was the only one left.

"What is that idiotic goat doing now?" exclaimed Scratch. "Great cans of fish! He's stepping up onto the platform!"

"Oh, mercy! I can't bear it!" cried Mrs. Alabaster. She collapsed onto the floor beside Palmer.

There was a breathless silence below as Scratch

peered ahead intently. "The three human beings on the platform appear puzzled," she said. "Oh! Oh! They seem to be looking around to see if Socrates has anyone with him. Well, he's done for now! No—now they're examining *him* just as they did the other goats. And what's this, for cat's sake? They're hanging a blue ribbon around his neck."

"Mercy! What's that?" asked Mrs. Alabaster.

"Do you know what it is, Clyde? Do you know?" asked Fringe.

"No sir, can't say that I do," said Clyde.

"Well, whatever it is, from the look on his face, I have a feeling there'll be no living with him after this!" With what seemed just one long graceful leap, Scratch was back down beside the others.

"If he gets back!" said Clyde, shaking his head.

"Oh, he'll be back all right," Scratch said. "Other animals are going up on the platform now, and the human beings with goats are too busy with their own animals to bother with Socrates."

Scratch was right. Moments later, Socrates walked through the tent flap, the blue ribbon dangling from his neck.

Scratch sat down, raised an indifferent hind leg into the air, and began giving herself a bath. "Well, what happened to *you?*" she asked carelessly.

"Why, I believe I have just won first prize, in the form of a blue ribbon, for being the finest ex-

ample of goat at the fair!" said Socrates. He had a dazed expression on his face.

"Mercy!" said Mrs. Alabaster. "A blue ribbon! None of us has ever won a blue ribbon before, not for anything. Think of it!"

Even Scratch, for all her attempts at appearing unconcerned, could not disguise the look of admiration on her face. It was easy to see that she approved of Socrates' courage, if not his modesty.

But as Palmer trailed along with the other animals behind the crates once more to await nightfall, he was in despair. A blue ribbon, of all things! What was that pathetic scrap of silk going to do for them where they were heading? Someday, if he lived that long and had any grandchildren, he would tell them this strange little story. But then, they probably wouldn't believe it.

VIII / The Egg

If a kitten's not left behind,
should an egg be?
Should it, Clyde?

From THE THOUGHTS OF FRINGE

When the last tinny notes of the merry-go-round faded out over the fairground, and the last light bulb strung from the Ferris wheel blinked out like a dying star in the late summer night, the animals set out once again. With the judging now over, the goats had been taken from the tent, and there was no food put out for them. Still, the animals found some water left in the bowls, and they feasted at the trash barrels dotting the fairground, all of them overflowing with food deliciously warm and well-seasoned from sitting in the hot sun.

Scratch and Little Cleo licked not-quite-empty tuna cans; Socrates crunched sunbaked apple cores and greasy potato-chip sacks; Clyde, Fringe, and Palmer devoured the leftover crusts from ham-and-Swiss-cheese sandwiches; Mrs. Alabaster pecked at butter-soaked popcorn. It was altogether a splendid feast, and a temptation to stay longer. But it was only a wish, not a choice. They knew they had to leave. Still, their stomachs were fuller, their hearts were lighter, and a large golden moon shone down on them from the sky.

The going was a little easier, too. They found themselves on a pleasant dirt road that appeared to be deserted. House lights twinkled far in the distance, but there was nothing close by to worry them, no cars or trucks speeding past. There were only themselves and an occasional timid cricket who stopped its singing only to start up again as soon as they had passed it by. The grass and weeds by the side of the road felt soothing underfoot. There was a feeling of peace in the soft summer air.

But all at once, the deep silence of the country night was shattered.

"Mercy! I've found an egg! There's an egg lying right here by the road! It's mine! It's mine! Finders, keepers!"

"Where, Mrs. Alabaster?"

"My dear friends, it seems to me that—"

"Oh, do be still, Socrates! I see it. There it is!"

"Well sir, it looks like an egg, all right."

"Are you certain it's a duck egg, Mrs. Alabaster?"

"I don't care if it is or it isn't. Mercy, I'm not going to leave an egg sitting right out in the middle of—in the middle of—*here!*"

"Well, what are we going to do about it? We can't leave *you* right out in the middle of here either!"

"Well sir, someone will have to carry it."

"But who, Clyde? Who can? You and I are noses. Scratch couldn't get it in her mouth. Mrs. Alabaster can't carry an egg in her bill, and Socrates already has his mouth filled with Little Cleo. Who, Clyde, who?"

A hesitant cricket chirped in reply, but it soon stopped, and its song was replaced with an uncomfortable silence.

"Well, I guess that leaves me!" Palmer was horrified to hear that it was his own voice speaking. "All right. I—I'll do it."

But his offer was greeted with a loud squawk and a terrified flapping of wings. "Oh, mercy, Palmer will eat it! Palmer eats eggs. He told me so once."

"Mrs. Alabaster, that was long ago," Clyde said gently. "Palmer also told you that he would never eat another egg."

"Oh, mercy!" said Mrs. Alabaster faintly.

Palmer turned to the frightened duck. "Socrates promised to guard Little Cleo with his life, Mrs. Alabaster. I promise to do the same for your egg!"

Mrs. Alabaster began to sob and moan softly. "My egg! My egg! Don't let anything happen to my egg!"

Palmer plodded over to the egg, which lay in a clump of clover. It looked warm and protected, as if someone had loved it very much. He trembled a little. After all, this was the first time he would have an egg in his mouth that he didn't intend to crush with one stroke of his jaws. He was glad that his stomach was so full. This was going to be a real test, to cradle an egg gently in his mouth until they came to the forest.

He put his nose up close to it. He smelled it. He smelled it again. It didn't seem to have that familiar egg smell to it. Then he picked it up gingerly with his teeth. It had a curious heaviness that made his teeth feel as if they were cracking. He set the egg down and tried picking it up from a different side. It felt just as bad, hard and heavy as—as—a rock!

It *was* a rock, nothing but a white egg-shaped rock! Palmer knew it now, and that was what he had promised to guard with his life for Mrs. Alabaster. The poor foolish duck, so addled with wanting an egg that she could make a mistake like this! Palmer didn't want to hurt her by telling her, but she would have to be hurt someday anyway. And if he did carry the rock in his teeth all the miles and miles into the forest, then wouldn't he be just as idiotic as—well, as Socrates and his silly blue ribbon?

Palmer set the rock back down in its nest of clover. "Mrs. Alabaster—" he began.

"Oh, my egg! My egg! My precious egg!" she whispered. Her eyes, in the moonlight, were soft and moist with love.

"Mrs. Alabaster, your egg will be perfectly safe with me," Palmer said. He picked the rock up gently in his jaws once more, and the animal caravan moved on.

IX / *The Barn*

A very pleasant place, is a barn.

From THE THOUGHTS OF SCRATCH

"Oh, couldn't we stop so I could sit on my egg?" Mrs. Alabaster murmured plaintively over and over again.

"Mrs. Alabaster," Scratch said at last in a voice bristling with weariness, "Palmer is taking excellent care of your egg. I shouldn't be surprised to see it hatch right in his mouth. After all, I'm perfectly content to let Socrates carry Little Cleo. You don't hear me begging to sit on *her*, do you?"

For a while after this, there was only a hurt silence.

It was nearly daybreak, and a heavy early morning mist rose up from ground damp with dew. Night crickets had long since stopped singing. Up ahead, the two dogs raised their heads to the sky, whining to each other as they looked from side to side for a deep ditch, a grove of trees, anyplace where they could hide before the sun rose. As a faint gray light spread across the sky, their search began to seem more and more hopeless. And then, suddenly, what they had all thought was simply a low-hanging cloud became a barn as they drew near it.

None of them remembered ever having been in a barn before, so at first they weren't quite certain that that's what it was. However, as they walked hesitantly in, guided by moonlight shining through the wide doors, Socrates whispered, "My dear friends, it *is* a barn! I was born in one, you know. Of course, I don't remember much about it because I was only a kid then." He looked a bit crestfallen that no one admired his joke.

They were all too busy taking in the soaring rafters, the lofts spilling over with hay, the stalls, the pens, the coops, the cages; breathing in the thick rich smells of old wood and leather, sweet straw and oats, and sleeping animals; and wondering just what they should do with themselves next. Then a cow's voice spoke to them gently from the darkness.

"Welcome to our barn! May I do anything to help you?"

Clyde whined and padded over to her stall. "There are seven of us—myself, another dog, a cat and her kitten, a goat, a duck, and a skunk—all needing a place to hide for the day. Have you such a hiding place here?"

There was a slight pause, and then the cow said hesitantly, "Did you say *skunk?*"

"He is one of our family of animals," Clyde replied simply.

"I see," said the cow. She thought a moment further. "Well, there is an empty stall right next to me, once occupied by an old friend of mine, a plowhorse. The stall is used only for winter storage now, and is rarely entered in the summer. I'm certain you will be quite safe there until nightfall. But if you will excuse me for asking"—the cow hesitated again—"where do you come from, and where do you go?"

Clyde exchanged glances with the other Patch animals before speaking. "We are running away from a family that no longer wants us," he said, "and we go to the forest to hide so that we can stay together."

"The forest?" said the cow with surprise. "The —the duck, too?"

"The duck, too," said Clyde.

The cow shook her head. "Poor soul!"

Mrs. Alabaster, anxious eyes fastened on her egg in Palmer's jaws, fortunately did not hear the remark.

"Is the forest anywhere near?" Clyde asked quickly.

"Oh, yes," replied the cow. "Once you have crossed the pasture, gone through the wire fence, which is no barrier for small animals such as you are, and crossed a wide dry ditch, you will have only a short distance to go before you come to the first trees. But are you all certain the forest is where you want to go?"

"Quite certain," said Clyde. Then he cleared his throat in a rather apologetic manner.

"Is there something else?" inquired the cow.

"We are hungry and thirsty," said Clyde.

"Why, of course you are!" said the cow in a soft, soothing, sympathetic voice. "You will find a tank filled with fresh water just outside the barn door. Not too far from my stall is a rabbit hutch, and there are always lettuce leaves and carrot tops fallen to the ground around it. Chicken and duck feed is scattered everywhere on the barn floor, and you will also find a large bowl of dog biscuits placed here for the dogs who are presently asleep in the farmhouse. I'm sorry that there is nothing we can offer the cat and her kitten, however, as our cats are generally fed in the kitchen, or they forage for themselves."

While this conversation was going on, Scratch began to pace the barn floor restlessly, her head lifted, her narrowed eyes watching. Then, suddenly, without anyone having actually seen her leave, she was a silent shadow, soaring into the rafters high over their heads. Soon she returned with a large rat dangling from her mouth. Scratch the wanderer! Scratch the hunter! Clyde and Fringe and Socrates looked at her with proud eyes.

"Please help yourselves to all you can find," the gentle cow said.

After Clyde had thanked the cow for all her kind help, the animals ate and drank, accompanied only by the dusky early morning silence of the barn. But as they started for the empty stall, a cluster of ducks, out for an early forage, waddled complacently through the barn door. They were led by a large, handsome duck whose feathers gleamed a soft milky white through the near darkness. Suddenly the barn exploded with the stormy sound of wings flapping wildly and birds screeching.

"Skunk! Skunk! Egg eater! Egg eater!" The smaller ducks squawked and shrieked from behind the safety of the large duck, who simply stood and stared.

But before Palmer could set the rock down from

his mouth and tell the ducks they had nothing to fear from him, Mrs. Alabaster had turned to them and said in a chilling voice, "This skunk is my friend. He does not eat the eggs of ducks." Then she exclaimed indignantly under her breath, "Mercy! What a silly fuss! Come along, Palmer." Without a backward look, she waddled on her way to the stall with the other Patch animals, leaving only Palmer to see the look of admiration in the eyes of the large duck.

Inside the stall, Mrs. Alabaster's bright black eyes darted this way and that, looking for a suitable place for her egg. She soon discovered a nest of old straw far in the corner. Palmer plodded over behind her and laid the rock in the nest, as gently as if it were made of snail gloss and cobwebs. Then he collapsed in a weary heap right where he stood, his jaws aching, as Mrs. Alabaster climbed on the nest and settled herself comfortably on the rock. Soon she began making soft crooning sounds in her throat and singing the rock-egg a lullaby.

Dear little egg,
Lovely egg of my own,
Safe under my wing,
You have found a home.

Sleep tight, little egg,
So pure and so white,
In your feathery nest,
Good night, good night.

The noisy ducks had by now calmed down and moved away, and a deep peace and quiet fell in the barn once more. But for some reason, Palmer could not drop off to sleep. Thoughts kept thumping through his head, one leaving only because it had been nudged out by another, like raindrops off a leaf.

Once again he began to wonder what he was doing with this bunch of animals. So far they had had the wildest kind of luck—a pond in a park, a tent at a fair, a comfortable stall in a barn—all lulling them into a false feeling of safety. But soon would come the forest, and what then for a goat whose first line of defense was a pitiful scrap of blue ribbon around his neck; for a skunk with no defense at all; for a tiny kitten, two tail-wagging dogs whose every thought had been directed by human beings, and a duck, the natural prey of half the animals of the forest, now crooning lullabies to a rock? True, there was a cat, a born hunter, who had just captured a rat, but a rat was a long cry from a forest enemy. Palmer sighed and looked around at the animals in the stall with him, all peacefully asleep —Socrates snoring gently; Fringe curled up trustingly against his friend, Clyde; Little Cleo, a small dark hill beside her mother's paw; and Mrs. Alabaster, her head dropping over her nest as her last lullaby ended.

But all at once, as Palmer watched them, the oddest feeling came over him. Without knowing why he did it, he rose to his feet, and then slowly and painfully, because his feet now really did hurt almost as much as his jaws, he crept over to the sleeping animals and touched each one with his nose. Then he returned to Mrs. Alabaster's nest and dropped down beside it again.

The feeling he had confused and puzzled him. He was glad the other animals hadn't seen him doing this strange and funny thing. But now, for some reason, his brain seemed to quiet down, and he felt more peaceful. He took deep breaths of the calming smells of the old barn, mingled with the familiar and curiously comforting smells of goats and cats, dogs and duck, and told himself that at least he was safe that day. He could think about tomorrow when tomorrow came. And almost before that thought left his head, he was asleep.

X / *The Strange Animal*

See how she waddles! Oh, the
charm, the grace, the elegance!

From THE THOUGHTS OF MR. DUCK

Despite all the daytime noises in the
barn, Palmer awoke only once. That was to hear
the quiet voice of the cow relating the story of their
arrival. It didn't surprise him. He supposed that
most of the barn animals would be curious about
their story.

"What a brave creature!" he heard a duck ex-
claim softly. Palmer wondered in a drowsy sort of
way if it wasn't the large duck who had looked at
Mrs. Alabaster with such admiration.

After this, he drifted right back to sleep, and

the next thing he knew, Clyde was nudging his nose and whining. It was time for them to be on their way again.

Palmer rose and waited patiently for Mrs. Alabaster to climb down from her nest. Then he clamped his still-aching jaws around the rock and followed the other animals from the stall.

They found what food they could in the hushed, sleeping barn, then crept out to stand side by side before the water tank, taking long drinks. When they had drunk as much as they could, they set out across the barnyard.

Early that evening a wind had sprung up, and dark clouds scudded across the sky. But as the animals came to the edge of the barnyard, the moon hung like a pale green pumpkin between two clouds, lighting up the pasture and everything beyond it. In the distance, they could now see crowds of dark, shapeless giant silhouettes against the churning sky. As if they all belonged to one animal, hoofs, paws, and webbed feet hesitated and finally stopped.

"Is that the forest? Is it, Clyde?" Fringe asked.

Clyde whined softly. "Why, yes, Fringe, I believe it is. Our friend the cow did tell us the beginning of it was not far beyond the pasture."

"Oh, mercy, the forest!" said Mrs. Alabaster.

No one seemed able to move.

A spark from the moon's cold, clear light shot out from Scratch's eyes. "Well, isn't that what we came for?" she said in a voice that was velvet soft but had claws behind it. Without warning, she streaked forward in a sudden leap toward the pasture. Then she stopped to look over her shoulder at the others.

"My dear friends . . ." began Socrates, but for once he could think of nothing more to say.

Clyde lifted his head to the sky in what seemed to be a silent howl. Then his solid, sturdy form loosened and fell into motion as he loped forward to Scratch. Close behind him, like a small shadow, was Fringe. Only a moment passed before Socrates had Little Cleo in his mouth and was trotting after them. When they reached Scratch, they all stopped.

"Come along, Palmer. They are waiting for us," said Mrs. Alabaster.

Palmer picked up the rock once again.

How many times the moon came from behind a cloud and then disappeared again, before they had crossed the pasture, no one knew, but they came at last to the wire fence, just as the cow had told them they would. And also as she had told them, the fence was no barrier to small animals such as they were. Scratch flew through it as easily as a gust of wind. Socrates and Clyde stepped over the lower wire, then held it down for the others to walk over.

When they had crossed the wide dry ditch that bordered the pasture, the going grew harder. The pasture had been moist, cool, and soft underfoot, and it gave off the smells of familiar, friendly animals. Now the ground was softened by grass and weeds only in places. Small, sharp rocks and treacherous, slippery pebbles gave way underfoot. Then gradually the trees began, first one, then two and three; an oak here, a maple there, three pines farther on. The trees grew closer and closer together. Branches began to touch overhead like gnarled fingers, and finally to tangle and twist around each other. At last, when the animals turned to look back, the barn and the pasture had disappeared.

So now they were in the forest, Palmer told himself, alone and unprotected. Well, unprotected, yes. But were they really alone? He had almost forgotten how the forest sounded at night. The wind had died down now, but odd voices whispered through the branches overhead. A low branch, old and tired, snapped at them. A thick vine hissed as it slithered past. A strange animal cried out somewhere, but *where* somewhere? In the distance? Behind the next tree? A dry twig crackled under Palmer's foot, and his heart drummed against his chest with fear.

By now the dogs, who had been "noses" when they traveled by road, had given their place in the lead to Scratch, who became "eyes," cat's eyes that

could see in the deepness and the darkness of the forest. Yet even with Scratch's help, they stumbled along uncertainly, bumping into trees, tripping over tree roots and hidden rocks. At last Clyde whined and gave a soft, sharp bark. They all drew to a stop.

"What is it? What is it, Clyde?" Fringe asked.

Mrs. Alabaster's wings began to flutter weakly. "Oh, mercy, I'm so frightened!"

"My dear Mrs. Alabaster," spoke a quavering voice, "we must try to be brave."

"Oh, for cat's sake, Socrates, we're all being as brave as we can," Scratch said. The matter-of-fact sound of her voice had an instant soothing effect on Mrs. Alabaster, and her wings grew still. "Is something wrong, Clyde?" Scratch asked.

"Well sir," Clyde said thoughtfully, "it seems to me that since we're not traveling on human beings' roads any longer, and there aren't likely to be any human beings here, why then, why shouldn't we rest at night and travel by day? We've slept all day, that's true, but then we've come a long way, too, so why not stop here?"

"*Here?*" said Socrates.

"What's wrong with here?" said Scratch. "Isn't it as good as anyplace, Palmer?"

Palmer set down the rock. No place in the forest was good as far as he was concerned, but what was the point of saying so? "Yes, it's as good as any," he said, and tried to keep his voice from trembling.

"But how can we sleep?" asked Mrs. Alabaster. "Mercy! Who'll watch over us?"

Scratch darted for the nearest tree. Digging her claws into the bark, she seemed to flow up, rather than climb up. "I will, from here! You can take the watch later from down below, Clyde. Sleep warm!" They could see her white bib flash through a ray of moonlight as she leaped up into the branches.

A moment passed, and then another small white bib flashed up after her. It was Little Cleo, climbing her first tree.

"Come along, kitten!" Scratch's voice was filled with pride.

So Little Cleo was growing up now. And in growing up, she was finding new ways to use her claws, for climbing, and perhaps for protecting herself. He had had a weapon, too, Palmer reflected mournfully, and had learned to use it. But his had been taken away from him. And he couldn't even climb a tree! He was as helpless as—as a duck, and would be for the rest of his life.

With a silent sigh of despair, Palmer picked up the rock in his jaws and carried it to the nest of soft moss that Mrs. Alabaster had found between two tree roots. When she had settled herself over it, he dropped down beside her, resting his head on the forest floor.

Once the forest, with its moist mossy smells, its thick carpet of leaves and tumbling acorn cups, its chirping insects and singing birds, had been his home. Now it was a strange and terrifying place. As he listened to the forest voices calling to each other through the dark, he wondered if he could ever really sleep again. But when he saw the two dogs, their heads resting quietly on their paws, yet with eyes open and alert, and thought of Scratch hiding somewhere on a tree branch over his head, it made his heart stop thumping quite so hard and allowed his eyes to drift shut.

But suddenly his eyes flew open, and he stiffened with fear. Only a few trees away, something was crashing through the undergrowth! It was a terrible sound, a sound without fear that could come only from an animal so big, or one who had such a powerful weapon, that it was afraid of no one and didn't care who heard it.

Clyde and Fringe leaped up, whining, their bodies stiff.

"Stay here, kitten!" a voice hissed softly in the treetops. Silvery and graceful as falling rain, Scratch flew down the tree and darted over to stand beside the dogs.

Then out from behind a tree stepped the animal.

"Friends," it said; "dearest madam," it addressed Mrs. Alabaster, "I have heard your story with the greatest admiration, and if you will have me, I should like to join your brave party!"

It was the large, handsome duck from the farm.

"Mercy!" said Mrs. Alabaster.

XI / *The Forest*

*My dear friends, a forest can be
a fairy tale for an animal.*

From THE THOUGHTS OF SOCRATES

As with many farm animals, the duck had no name, but they could call him Mr. Duck, he told them cheerfully. At any rate, his coming seemed to raise everyone's spirits immensely. It didn't even matter that he was just as helpless as Mrs. Alabaster and might well be more of a burden than a benefit if there was danger. He was such a well-mannered, handsome fellow. Bold and brave, too, for hadn't he followed them alone through the dark forest?

It took some time for them to settle down

again after the excitement of Mr. Duck's arrival, but they did at last, and the rest of the night passed uneventfully. When they rose again, it was morning. Sunshine lay in peaceful pools on the forest floor. In a wild cherry tree nearby, a cardinal sang.

Mrs. Alabaster quacked, stood up from her nest, and stretched out her wings eagerly. Mr. Duck was at her side in a moment. From the way he looked at her, it was easy to see what had prompted him to join their brave band!

"Dear madam, did you have a pleasant rest?" he asked.

"Oh, mercy, yes!" replied Mrs. Alabaster happily, as Mr. Duck waddled over to see the egg.

Observing this, Palmer shook inside. Surely a farm duck would know the difference between an egg and a rock!

Mr. Duck stared at the egg, and then moved his head closer to stare at it again.

"Splendid, dear madam," he said. "Simply splendid!"

Palmer gave a sigh of relief. If Mr. Duck had noted anything strange about the egg, he apparently intended to say nothing about it.

Socrates was soon at work daintily nipping berries off a wild blackberry bush he had discovered. Both of the ducks and Palmer enjoyed a nice breakfast of insects they found crawling in the decaying stump of a tree. Only the two dogs and the cat and her kitten remained hungry.

"Never mind. We'll find meat later," Scratch said. And when they saw her scanning the treetops with narrowed eyes, they felt certain that food would not be a problem for anyone in the forest.

It was water that was needed. When they found water, Palmer told them, that was where they should settle. What he did not tell them was how difficult finding water might be. The pond in the park, the bowls in the goats' tent, the tank outside the barn—it had all been so splendid and simple. Still, he said nothing to dull the spirits of the others as they set out once more.

Little Cleo no longer wanted to be carried by Socrates. She wanted to walk with the rest. And to stop and play! Everything was a toy to her—a piece of dried bark, an insect skittering under a fallen leaf, a sunbeam. More than once Scratch cuffed her with a firm paw to keep her from straying.

Still, even for the older animals, the forest seemed to offer an endless string of delightful discoveries—clumps of lacy ferns; rocks softened by coats of pale gray-green lichen; nests of wild violets; strange plants and pebbles. But by the time the sun was straight overhead and pouring hotly on them through the trees, their high spirits had begun to droop. By late afternoon, when the sun had fallen below the treetops, they trudged along in silence and gloom. Little Cleo had long since begun to mew that she was tired, and she was once again in Socrates' mouth. It began to look as if there were no chance of their finding water before nightfall, if at all.

Time and again, Clyde thumped over to a thick-trunked tree to snuffle around its roots, or dug under a mound of rotting leaves, only to look up and shake his head. Nothing! Summer seemed to have dried up the whole forest.

At last Socrates set Little Cleo down. "My dear friends," he said, "I don't know if I can go on. My gullet is withered. There is a curious noise in my ears—"

"Well, you aren't the only one," Scratch said. Her voice sounded dry as sand.

A curious noise in everyone's ears, including his own! Palmer felt he should have recognized it at once—the hushed, whispering sound of a lazy forest stream. Carefully, he set the rock down on the ground. "It's water!" he said. His throat felt as if he had just swallowed a mouthful of parched timothy grass. "What we all have in our ears is the sound of running water!"

"My dear Palmer, it couldn't—" Socrates began.

But Scratch whirled on him. "Sssst!" she hissed.

She stood still as stone, listening.

Both dogs stiffened.

Then Scratch became alive again, and with one swift move, disappeared into the trees. The dogs hurtled after her. The others waited in watchful silence, until at last Scratch reappeared. In her green eyes was a dazed, wondering look.

"It is water," she said simply. Then she turned back into the trees.

It was only a small stream, but it was enough. Its cool, clear water flowed dreamily over a clean sandy bottom and moss-covered pebbles. Graceful long-legged insects skimmed over its surface. In its depths, minnows darted from secret hiding places behind the underwater grass. The animals stood beside the stream, dipped their heads down, and drank. They lifted their heads, then dipped and drank again. The long trailing branches of a willow tree drifted peacefully over them.

"Mercy!" The enchanted silence was shattered by a loud squawk from Mrs. Alabaster. "A pond!"

"My dear Mrs. Alabaster," said Socrates, "this is a stream. A pond is round and still. A stream is long and —"

"Dear madam, I believe you are absolutely right," Mr. Duck interrupted. "Mrs. Alabaster is absolutely right," he repeated for the benefit of the others. "There *is* a pond!"

What Mrs. Alabaster's bright eyes had found was a place just beyond them where water had flowed through a small passageway and settled in what must have been a dip in the ground. It was not a very large one, but even Socrates had to agree that it *was* a pond.

"I don't believe this!" said Palmer to himself. And before too long, he was to say the same thing again. And again!

The very next time was when they discovered, directly across the pond, an outcropping of boulders, and an opening between them that led to a small, but quite ample cave. A hundred forest animals could have already discovered it and made a home of it, yet there it was, empty and waiting for them.

And Palmer never stopped being amazed at how these backyard animals, whose only achievement in the matter of feeding themselves had been to learn the sound of a refrigerator door opening, were able to find food for themselves.

Scratch and Little Cleo turned out to be fine fishers. Their claws were as quicksilver swift as the slippery minnows they caught. And they climbed trees more silently than birds could cut through air.

Socrates satisfied his tastes on rare herbs and weeds, berries and mosses. Once again, his jaws rotated over something from dawn to dusk.

Mr. Duck and Mrs. Alabaster feasted on sow-bugs and tender earthworms, beetles and fur-coated caterpillars.

Only the dogs went hungry, and that was just at first. Awkward and clumsy, they splashed hel-ter-skelter into the stream, frightening the fish away. When they heard the small sounds made by *something* in the trees, they went crashing after it, only to slink back with their tails down and foolish looks on their faces because they'd caught nothing. But very quickly, though they never did become fishers, they did learn the need for stealth and si-lence when they were stalking their prey.

Prey! That was the one thought that never left Palmer's mind. Often he couldn't even look when Clyde or Fringe, Scratch or Little Cleo, came back from a hunt with something small and formerly alive dangling from the mouth. He really knew there was no other way. In the forest, it was eat or be eaten. And didn't he himself capture live food —small snakes and insects and mice, among other things? But seeing an animal in someone else's mouth was a constant reminder of how helpless he was. Or for that matter, how helpless they all were if the right enemy came along. And in time it would have to, Palmer knew, because the forest was alive with creeping, crawling, stalking, *hungry* enemies.

XII / *The Attack*

*Courage and character can't
always be measured by
conversations (especially the
conversations of an old goat).*

From THE THOUGHTS OF SCRATCH

Something else worried Palmer, too. That was Mrs. Alabaster's egg. He knew that one day he would have to tell her the truth about it, and the longer he put it off, the harder it would be.

On a cloudy gray afternoon, he sat watching her waddle cheerfully to her nest by the pond, and settle herself over the rock. The clouds reflected in the pond didn't seem to disturb her happiness in the least. Mr. Duck dove into the water and swam in wide circles in front of her, dipping his head and dipping again. Each time his head came up, the ducks made soft cooing sounds to one another. But no time was ever a good time to talk to Mrs. Alabaster, Palmer had discovered, so it might just as well be now as later. He waited until Mr. Duck decided to take a sail to the opposite side of the pond, and then he started his unpleasant journey to Mrs. Alabaster.

Halfway to her nest, he heard a dry twig snap behind him. That would be Clyde or Fringe or Scratch or Little Cleo, coming back from a hunt, Palmer told himself. He turned, expecting to see one or the other coming through the undergrowth with a limp something hanging from the mouth. It would not be Socrates, he knew, because the goat was presently snoring peacefully behind the boulders of their cave. Still, the presence of any animal meant he would have to give up his talk with Mrs. Alabaster until another time. He waited, but none of the animals appeared through the trees. He waited a moment longer. And in that moment, he saw in the tangled darkness of a mat of wild vines the two barest pinpricks of light. Another look told him the pinpricks of light came from the evil slanted eyes of a fox!

Palmer felt the fur rise on his neck and his heart begin to thud in his chest as he inched forward, and felt the narrow, deadly eyes inching along with him. Curiously, it was not himself he was thinking of at that moment. It was a white duck sitting on a nest, a duck who might very well lose her life trying to protect a rock!

But how to get Mrs. Alabaster off the nest and into the pond where she would be safe? And how to do it quickly before the fox attacked? There was one possible way. He raised his tail in the direction of the fox as if he were preparing to use his weapon. At the same time, he cried out, "Mrs. Alabaster! Danger! Danger! Fox! Get into the pond! Run! Jump!"

But the bewildered duck only fluttered her wings helplessly. "Where? Where?"

"Never mind!" shrieked Palmer. "Just run!"

"But I can't leave my egg!" cried Mrs. Alabaster. "I won't leave my precious egg!"

Now Palmer had to say it. There was no time to wait. At any moment now, the fox would discover that a raised tail, the raised tail of *this* skunk, at any rate, meant nothing. Palmer edged closer to the nest, and with his tail still curled high over his back, he said in as gentle a voice as he could, "Mrs. Alabaster, your egg isn't an egg at all. It's only a rock! Please go to the pond!"

And then from the pond came the stern voice of Mr. Duck. "Dear madam, Palmer is right. The egg is only a rock. Please come into the pond at once!"

"A rock? It couldn't be a rock!" Mrs. Alabaster stood up weakly, only to collapse onto her nest again.

"Mrs. Alabaster," Palmer said, "I will guard whatever it is with my life. Listen to Mr. Duck, and *go!*" To his relief, Mrs. Alabaster rose again and, half waddling, half falling down the shallow embankment, swam out into the pond.

At the same moment, Palmer heard the sound of leaves crunching behind him, and he turned to see the fox creeping forward. Suspicion gleamed in the fox's sly, slanted, wicked eyes. As he drew closer, his eyes began to burn with small red fires of hatred. He knew now that he had been taken in, bluffed, made a fool of. His body tensed as he made ready to lunge at Palmer.

And then Palmer opened his jaws. His jaws! Jaws that had been strong enough to carry a rock for miles and miles without dropping it once. Powerful skunk jaws! In his despair at losing one weapon, Palmer had forgotten that he had another one, one just as good, just as deadly, as that of any fox! The sight of the open jaws stopped the fox for a moment. He remained tense, but he simply stood staring at Palmer with fiery eyes.

"It isn't a rock! Palmer is wrong. It's an egg, and I'm going back to it!" The tearful voice of

Mrs. Alabaster sailed across the smooth surface of the pond.

Palmer heard it, and it was then that he made his mistake. It was a mistake no forest animal should ever make. He turned his head. It was for only a quick moment to look toward Mrs. Alabaster, but the fox took the moment and shot forward. Palmer felt a blinding pain as the fox sank thorn-sharp teeth into his right front leg, piercing the flesh and going deep into the bone. Palmer opened his jaws, snapped, and snapped again. But he knew, just as the fox knew, that he was weaker already, that the pain was tearing at him, that he was finished. The fox backed away, ready to lunge again.

And just then, a calm, dignified voice spoke out to them from somewhere near the boulders. "My dear animal," it said smoothly, "if you do not cease your abominable attack at once, I shall take measures that will make you rue the day you set foot near our home!"

The fox lifted his head in surprise.

"You heard what the goat said!" hissed a cat's voice from somewhere in the treetops.

"Yes sir, you certainly did!" growled the voice of a large dog.

"You've got ears just like the rest of us!" barked a dog in a voice that was small, but just as determined as the others.

The fox hesitated, then tensed once more for a second attack.

"Very well, have it your own way," said the goat calmly. "One, two, three, everyone!" Then he lowered his horns, and with a scrap of blue ribbon waving from his neck like a banner, charged at the fox.

At the same moment, a snarling cat came flying from the tree tops, her claws outstretched, while two dogs with fangs bared hurtled out from the under-growth.

The fox never had a chance, and he soon knew it. Buffeted and bruised by the goat's horns, scratched and scraped by the cat's claws, ripped and torn by the dogs' fangs, he was tossed and rolled from trees to cave to the brink of the pond like a helpless fur ball. His eyes were soon swollen, his ears in shreds. He was whipped and miserable. At the very first moment he saw of escape, he slunk away with his tail tucked between his legs, lucky to get off with his life.

But by now the pain in Palmer's leg was a raging fire. He barely saw the fox make his escape. And for some idiotic reason, he had only one thought in his head—the egg!

"Mrs. Alabaster's egg!" he gasped. "Is it all right?"

He saw Clyde run to the nest, sniff the rock,

and finally test it with his teeth. Then the strangest look came over Clyde's face. That was the last thing Palmer saw before a great burst of pain shot up his leg and all through his body, and everything went black.

XIII / *The Last Decision*

Well sir, there are some things
no animal can do.
It has to be faced.

From THE THOUGHTS OF CLYDE

From that moment on, Palmer's life was nothing but times when his whole body was hot and hurting, strung together by times when he drifted back into darkness. He was in the cave, he knew, where somehow he had been dragged by the others. And in the times when he was not in darkness, he always felt one of the animals licking his swollen leg—Scratch mostly, he thought, but often Clyde or Fringe. Sometimes it was even Little Cleo. Around him, he could hear hushed, anxious voices.

One voice, above the others, he heard over and

over, saying the same things. "Poor Palmer! Risking his life for me! And carrying that rock, when all the time he knew it wasn't an egg! He wanted to spare me, and I wasn't worth sparing. What a foolish creature I've been! Oh, Mr. Duck! Oh, everyone! Please help Palmer!"

Palmer tried to speak, to tell Mrs. Alabaster that she wasn't a foolish creature at all, but he couldn't even open his jaws, and again and again, he went back into darkness. Palmer lost all track of how often he drifted in and out of the darkness. Then at last he heard Socrates say:

"My dear friends, Palmer is not getting any better. In fact, he is, as we all can see, growing much worse. If we don't do something soon, I fear that—" The speech ended in a choking sound.

"Well then," Scratch said softly, "let's *do* something!"

"Mercy, if our family were only here, they'd *do* something!" moaned Mrs. Alabaster.

An ironclad silence greeted this remark.

"Mrs. Alabaster," Clyde said gently, "we have no family but ourselves now. Yet that isn't to say we can't see human beings again."

"What do you mean? What do you mean by that, Clyde?" Fringe asked.

"Well sir, what I mean is that human beings are the only ones who can help Palmer now. In matters of food and water and fighting off enemies, we've been able to take care of ourselves. Oh, maybe we haven't done so well as when we were backyard animals, and maybe we've missed our—our human beings more than any of us has said, but we've managed. But this is something else altogether. This is something we *can't* manage. And I don't think we should be ashamed to admit that we need human beings to help Palmer, or else there's no telling what might happen to him!"

"Mercy!" sobbed Mrs. Alabaster.

"But if we find human beings, Clyde," Fringe said, "we might end up getting separated. Isn't that right, Clyde?"

"That's right," Clyde said. "That's why I'm asking all of you to decide what to do. We all have to say it, not just one of us—whether we find human beings to help Palmer, or wait here until—"

"Dear friends," Socrates interrupted, "perhaps we *could* return to our—to the same human beings. Perhaps they're not angry with us any longer. Anyway, maybe all this time we've been mistaken, and they weren't going to give us away or separate us."

"They may not be angry any longer about those other things we did," Scratch retorted, "but the picture has changed now. We ran away. What human beings would want back animals who had run away?"

"Scratch is right," Clyde said. "We can't go back again. If we look for human beings, it has to be other human beings. Maybe we might even find someone who would keep us all. But we can't count on anything. Being separated is what we'll have to count on."

Being separated? He wouldn't let them do that, Palmer's brain told him through a painful haze. He must stop them! But again, he couldn't make the words come out. He could only lie there and hear the voices say:

"So we'll count on that! But I agree with Clyde, that we'll have to find human beings."

"My dear friends, of course we must!"

"Well sir, you already know my feelings."

"I feel that way, too, Clyde!"

"Mercy, yes!"

"There is no other way, dear madam!"

And those were the last words Palmer heard before he went into a long, long darkness.

XIV / *The Ending*

*Is everything going to be
all right? Is it, Clyde?*

From THE THOUGHTS OF FRINGE

Palmer awoke from a long deep sleep
to find that his eyes were clear and the terrible
pain was gone. He felt weak and rather tired, and
his brain was still a little fuzzy, but he didn't hurt
anymore, not anywhere. There was something curious about his leg, though. It was all wrapped in
something white, and it stuck out like a small,
straight twig. He couldn't bend it when he tried.

He saw that he was in a box without a top on it,
and with a large opening cut in one side. Under
him was a kind of nest of something red and yellow
and blue and soft and comfortable. The box wasn't

in their cave, however, but in a very small room that reminded him somehow of the toolshed where Scratch's kittens had been born. Far over his head a clump of oak leaves brushed against a tiny dusty window. The leaves were turning yellow. Was it becoming autumn already? Palmer wondered lazily.

But where were his friends? Why weren't they all here to see how much better he was? Where could they be? Then, as Palmer's thoughts grew clearer and clearer, his heart began to thump. Had the animals found help for him, only to be given away, separated from each other just as they had expected? But perhaps they were still someplace nearby. The door to his little room was open, Palmer saw. If only he could get to it! He must warn them. He must tell them not to worry about him, to leave at once, to run away to their home in the forest.

He was so weak, and his right front leg was so stiff in its white wrapping, that it seemed an endless struggle to climb from the box and begin the slow, clumsy crawl to the door. And then, before he could even get halfway across the floor, heavy footsteps approached, and a young man with a pleasant tanned face, wearing the same kind of blue cotton trousers and rubber-soled shoes that Jonathan Patch used to wear, came striding into the room.

"Well, I'll be darned!" he said softly. "Carol!

Carol!" he called out the door. "Our skunk is up, and he's walking!"

It seemed as if he had hardly finished speaking before a young woman with a bright pink bandana around her head rushed into the room. She took only a moment to put down the garden trowel in her hand and to brush clumps of wet mud off her bare knees before she kneeled down beside Palmer.

"I thought for a moment you were teasing me, Steve," she said.

"Would I tease about a thing like this? By the way, where are the rest of them? I thought they'd be right behind you."

Carol laughed and pointed over her shoulder. "They are!" she said, as in through the door trooped Scratch, Clyde, Fringe, Socrates, Little Cleo, Mrs. Alabaster, and Mr. Duck.

"I wonder if the little fellow knows how lucky he is to be alive," Steve said, stooping down and patting Palmer's head. "I wouldn't be surprised if the others did. Do goats smile, do you think? If I didn't know better, that's what I'd say this one was doing."

"I don't know," Carol said. "But I do know that if these two dogs aren't careful, they're going to wag their tails right off! And listen to the way the cats are purring and the ducks cooing. Don't you think all this calls for a celebration?"

"You bet! Have we got anything to celebrate *with?*"

"Would you settle for two steak bones, a large can of tuna, a box of—"

"Well, what are we waiting for?" Steve broke in. "Let's bring on the party!"

The two of them had no sooner left the room than the talking and the explaining and the exclamations began. No one seemed to be able to get the words out fast enough. And yet when everything had settled down, there was still one subject that had not been mentioned. It was Palmer, finally, who had to bring it up.

"Will we be able to stay here together?" he asked. "Is it going to be a home for us all?"

The other animals exchanged solemn glances. "Well sir," Clyde said, "the fact is that nothing's been said about it."

"Then you've got to run away again!" Palmer blurted out. "Never mind about me. I'll be all right, but you've got to leave *now!*"

They were all silent as Scratch drew her pink tongue over a paw several times, then examined the paw studiously. This time it was not trembling. "We've all agreed to wait for you, Palmer," she said softly. "We'll take our chances."

And no matter what Palmer said about it, they wouldn't change their minds.

As it turned out, they didn't have to wait very

long to see what was going to happen to them. That
same afternoon, a laughing Steve and Carol opened
the garden gate, and behind them stood Mr. and
Mrs. Patch and Jonathan! Tears streamed down
Mrs. Patch's face, and Mr. Patch was busy doing
something to his own with a large white handker-
chief. Nobody could tell *what* was happening with
Jonathan, because he flew through the gate so fast
that the animals *felt* him long before they really
saw him. He was trying to throw his arms around
all of them at the same time.

Laughing and crying, Mr. and Mrs. Patch ran
behind him to the animals, and for a long time
there was nothing but more laughter and tears,
joyful barks and quacks and purrs, hugs and pats
and scratches behind the ears. And when it had all
quieted down at last, there was a tall pitcher of
iced lemonade, warm gingerbread brought out in
the backyard by Carol and Steve, and more
explanations.

"Tell us again how you found them," Jonathan
pleaded. He was sitting on the grass with Little
Cleo purring on his lap, and Fringe curled in a
ball in front of him, trying to get as close to his
sneakers as it was possible to get.

Mrs. Patch leaned over to stroke Clyde's head.
"I can't tell you how wonderful all this is for us!"

"You don't have to," Steve said. "We can see
it!"

Clyde's tail thump, thumped on the ground, and Mrs. Patch laughed. "Oh, it's so good to hear that sound again!"

Scratch was stretched out on the arm of a wicker chair beside Mr. Patch, who was absently rubbing her chin, just as if they were back home together in his old faded armchair reading the morning newspaper like any other morning of the year. The only difference now was the dazed, happy look on Mr. Patch's face. "You know, Jonathan just hasn't been fit to live with," he said.

"Well, neither have you," said Mrs. Patch. "Neither have any of us!"

Carol stood up to refill lemonade glasses. The ice made a cool chinking sound as it fell from the pitcher. "You go ahead and tell the story, Steve," she said. "I've talked enough!"

"Well," Steve said, "as we mentioned before, it all began late one night when Carol and I were finishing up a game of Scrabble and getting ready to turn in, when we heard this scratching at the front door."

"Correction!" Carol broke in. "*You* heard it, Steve. I thought it was mice," she said apologetically.

"Well, it doesn't matter," said Steve, "because the fact is we both let them in."

"Let who in?" asked Jonathan eagerly.

"Now, don't interrupt, Jonathan."

"It was the dog and the cat at the door, the ones you call Clyde and Scratch. Well, it didn't take too much brilliance to see that they were anxious about something. Clyde was whining, and the two of them kept coming up to us, then running off a bit, then coming up to us again. There was no mistaking that they were trying to get us to go with them, so we finally did. We were pretty certain that somebody was in trouble."

"And somebody certainly was!" Carol exclaimed.

"They led us right to Palmer," Steve went on. "He was lying in a small cave, his right front leg all banged up. He was pretty far gone. Carol and I don't think he would have lasted more than two or three days if his friends hadn't come for help. Anyway, we brought the whole bunch home with us, and after we'd had Palmer taken care of by the vet, we began wondering where they all could have come from."

"We couldn't find an ad in the newspaper under *lost*," Carol said, "so we finally decided to put one in under *found*."

"And are we glad you did!" exclaimed Mr. Patch. "We stopped advertising because we weren't getting any calls. We only heard about your ad by accident. Our neighbors were taking care of a cat called Max for friends of theirs. When the friends came to collect Max, they happened to mention your ad. One thing led to another, and here we are!"

Steve shook his head. "It beats me why they ran away in the first place. Anyone could see that they had good care and a lot of love."

"Well, *I* know why they ran away!" Jonathan burst out. "It's because they thought we were going to give them all away. They didn't know it was only until we got settled in our new home. I told Mother and Dad we ought to explain things to them. They know animals can understand just about anything!"

Mr. Patch grinned sheepishly. "As a matter of fact, we *do* feel that way."

"That's okay," Carol said. "Steve and I feel that way, too."

"But the silly part is," said Mrs. Patch, "that my husband decided not to accept the new job, so we're not leaving after all. We're going to be staying right where we are, animals and all!"

"There are several things, though, that I still don't understand," said Mr. Patch. "That second duck, for one thing. Where did *he* come from? There was just Mrs. Alabaster when they left home, and now it seems there's a Mr. Alabaster, too."

"We have no idea," Steve told him. "All we

know is that he was with them when we found Palmer."

"And where did Socrates win that first prize?" Mr. Patch continued. "It's badly beaten up, but I know a first prize blue ribbon when I see one."

Mrs. Patch sighed. "I guess we'll never know."

Steve and Carol grinned at each other. "Well, there's one thing you'll know!" Carol said.

"What's that?" asked Mrs. Patch.

"You're going to be taking something new home with you besides Mr. Alabaster. Come along. Your Mrs. Alabaster has something to show you."

They all trooped over to a flat wooden box by the back doorsteps. The box was lined with a nest of straw. And in the center of the nest was an egg, a real duck egg.

"Well, I declare!" said Mrs. Patch.

Then Carol insisted that they have more glasses of lemonade and at least one more slice of gingerbread for Jonathan before they left.

"Oh dear," said Mrs. Patch with a rueful laugh as they all sat back comfortably again in their chairs. "No matter what we do, we always seem to end up with another animal!"

At this remark, Jonathan's eyes flew open. "Does that mean we're going to keep Mr. Alabaster and Little Cleo, too?"

Mr. and Mrs. Patch smiled at one another. Then

Mrs. Patch threw out her hands and shrugged. "Well, why not?" she said, adding with a laugh, "And a duckling as well, I suppose!"

"Wow!" said Jonathan.

For a few moments, there were only the sounds of ice clinking in glasses and Clyde's leg thumping on the ground as he discovered a new flea.

Then all at once, Mr. Patch said, "Look, everyone! What do you suppose Palmer's up to?"

With his little wrapped leg sticking stiffly out in front, Palmer had suddenly started on a slow, but determined march toward Jonathan. Step, thump! Step, thump! He finally arrived at where Jonathan sat on the grass, and put his nose against Jonathan's leg. Then he turned and limped over first to Mrs. Patch, and then to Mr. Patch, touching both of their ankles with his nose. After that, he collapsed by Mr. Patch's feet.

"Well, what was all that about?" said Mrs. Patch.

"You know something?" Mr. Patch said. "This old fellow has changed. I don't know what's been happening to him, besides having that leg of his chewed up, but he would never have done anything like this before. He was always hanging around by himself in the backyard. Come to think of it, all of our animals seem to have changed a little, but especially Palmer. We'll never know what it was, but whatever happened to him, it must have been good." Mr. Patch leaned down to rub Palmer's ear gently. "Welcome home, Palmer Patch!" he said.

Palmer just sat there and enjoyed the luxury of having his ear rubbed. And then, quite suddenly, he laid his head down on Mr. Patch's scuffed leather moccasins and dropped soundly off to sleep, right there in front of everybody.

About the Author

Like the Patch family's pets, the Wallace family's pets are important parts of the household. They are, in fact, well-loved members of the family. And Barbara Wallace's special appreciation of animals and their individual personalities extends beyond her own feathered and four-footed family; she once sent a friend's puppy a hand-monogrammed beach towel because "doesn't every California dog need one?"

PALMER PATCH is Mrs. Wallace's seventh book for Follett. It was first written about nine years ago, then shelved and forgotten by everyone except her husband, Jim, who loved all the foolish backyard animals, especially Mrs. Alabaster.

"Jim never let up on the book, and never let me beg off in the discouraging moments I had after I started reworking it," remembers Mrs. Wallace. "Most husbands (or wives) get an early book dedicated to themselves, but Jim always said he didn't want any book but *this* one. I feel that the whole Patch crew owe their lives to Jim, not to me. This is *his* book!"

Mrs. Wallace and her husband, their teenage son, Jimmy, and the family pets live in Alexandria, Virginia.